When I Forgot

ELINA HIRVONEN is a film maker and a journalist. This is her first novel.

DOUGLAS ROBINSON is an English professor and translator of Finnish literature whose debut novel, *Saarikoski's Spirits*, is being published first in Finnish translation.

From the reviews of *When I Forgot*:

'An exemplary first novel… a book that whets your appetite for another one.' *Spectator*

'This first novel is a slim but well-formed volume. At 180 pages it's a day's read, although many of the evocative situations Hirvonen conjures will remain in the mind for a lot longer.' *The List*

'This apparently unpretentious book is in fact a sophisticated response to 9/11 and a delicately woven meditation on love and war.' *TLS*

'At once both forceful and heart-rending. Hirvonen writes calmly and lucidly, and this short novel is accessible to a worldwide audience. An exciting author, and I for one greatly look forward to her next novel.' *The Book Depository*

'Compelling.' *Yorkshire Post*

When I Forgot

Elina Hirvonen

Translated by
Douglas Robinson

Portobello
BOOKS

First published by Portobello Books Ltd 2007
This paperback edition published 2008

Portobello Books Ltd
Twelve Addison Avenue
Holland Park
London W11 4QR, UK

First published in Finland by Avain Publishers in 2005

The translation of this book has been supported by FILI,
the Finish Literature Information Centre.

A CIP catalogue record is available from the British Library

9 8 7 6 5 4 3 2 1

ISBN 978 1 84627 095 6

www.portobellobooks.com

Designed and typeset in Columbus
by Patty Rennie

Printed in the UK by CPI Bookmarque, Croydon, CR0 4TD

Canst thou, O cruel! say I love thee not,

When I against myself with thee partake?

Do I not think on thee, when I forgot

Am of my self, all tyrant, for thy sake?

Who hateth thee that I do call my friend,

On whom frown'st thou that I do fawn upon,

Nay, if thou lour'st on me, do I not spend

Revenge upon myself with present moan?

What merit do I in my self respect,

That is so proud thy service to despise,

When all my best doth worship thy defect,

Commanded by the motion of thine eyes?

But, love, hate on, for now I know thy mind;

Those that can see thou lov'st, and I am blind.

William Shakespeare, Sonnet 149

To the End 1

To the end I felt pity that he was a child.
He should have been a cloud.
The kind birds hide in
when they're afraid.

Miltos Sachtouris

1

Why I'm happy

I'm happy because I have a steam engine (that works).

I'm happy because I have Daddy Mummy Sister Grandma and got a Stiiga sled for Christmas.

I'm happy because I'm in the science club and when I grow up I'm going to be an inventor and win the Nobel Prize.

I'm happy because I get to live my whole life in free and independent Finland and because my Heavenly Father loves me and takes care of me.

Joona Louhiniitty 3A

2

I can make it. This day.

There's the smell of sun-warmed dog shit and damp earth. A bent woman in winter boots from the eighties and a child in muddied waterproofs whose tongue darts out around his ice-cream moustache. There's the long morning when you don't have to look at your watch.

There's the café where you get old-fashioned coffee and thickly iced mocha squares and where you feel like someone's just told you a secret. There are the clacking trams and the foot-dragging kids on their way to school and the grey-headed women who prop each other up as they cross the street. There's the book I got from Ian. There's Ian, who loves me.

There's the book.

There's the world I am allowed to enter. Three women on a single day in different time periods. The writer Virginia Woolf, who filled her pockets with rocks and walked into the water.

You have been in every way all that anyone could be. I don't think two people could have been happier till this terrible disease came. I can't fight it any longer, I know that I am spoiling your life, that without me you could work.

I've read Virginia's suicide note many times, but keep coming back to it. What did the rocks look like? What was she thinking as she sank under the water? Did she have time, before losing consciousness, to regret what she had done?

3

I first saw Ian three years ago in a university lecture hall. He had been invited from Columbia University in New York as a visiting lecturer for the literature department's Virginia Woolf seminar. Ian was fortyish, but looked older. He was in brown corduroys and an orange-yellow sweater and the same kind of bumpy-soled health sandals that my mother wore when we were small. He stood in front of us looking thin and a bit hunched, a glass of water in one hand and a sheaf of paper in the other, turning his head back and forth looking for a place to set them down.

The girls in long skirts and the boys who pulled their wispy hair back into ponytails talked loudly about literature ('*Orlando* like totally expanded my sexuality, man') and last night's party ('So I wake up on some fucking tech student's floor and I'm like, uh, sorry') and Ian kept saying 'Excuse me, excuse me please' to get everybody to quiet down. Finally he set down the glass and the pile of paper, stamped his sandal and shouted 'Shut the fuck up!'

When Ian started to talk, we were all quiet. He sat on the table, pushed the papers aside, and took a sip of water. His gaze was intense and his voice deep and dark, as if someone were humming quietly just behind his words.

First Ian told us why he became a literary scholar. 'I'm convinced that it's important to remember. Only by remembering can we understand something about ourselves. But I happen to have a terrible memory. I wanted to fill in the gaps by stealing from others.' Ian looked away, took a drink from his glass, and began talking about this dazzlingly intelligent woman who lived a hundred years ago and who wanted to capture even the tiniest movements of the mind, to dive into a person's inner world in a way no-one had ever done in the history of world literature.

His voice tightened something in my throat. I wanted to raise my hand and tell him that remembering isn't really all that great. Memory is one of life's burdens that we can do nothing about. I wanted to stand up, make the note-taking and enthusiastic nods stop and shout that all I want is an escape from memory.

Ian's face flushed and his hands drew swoops in the air. His hands were thin and his wrists were hairy and I wanted to put my hand there too.

4

The phone rings before I get to the end of Virginia's letter.

'Where are you?' My mother's voice as doubting as ever.

'Transcribing an interview,' I lie. 'What?'

'Don't get angry. Could you please go see Joona?'

'I told you already. I want to make up my own mind when to go.'

'Yes, you told me. But it would mean a lot to Joona if you'd go now. He needs you. To get better.'

Oh, fuck off. That's what I want to say. Fuck off and let me live my own life for once. But you don't talk like that to your mother. Not any more, now that you're grown up and living in your own place. Not to the mother who has to care for Joona like some gigantic child. Not to the mother who in her whole life never had a door she could lock against other people's intrusions.

'Joona is not going to get better.'

'He could be less unhappy. He says you don't care about him any more.'

'Jesus Christ.'

'Joona asks about you all the time. What should I tell him?'

'You don't need to say anything. I'll go out there when I get this done.'

He says you don't care about him any more.

Where does he get off saying that? Where does he get off using a smarmy, crappy, hypocritical word like 'care'? Caring's been poisoned by children's songs and politicians. If only we could all just care about each other we'd all be happy happy happy.

But he's right, I don't care about Joona. What I feel for him is something else. Nothing warm or fuzzy or happy-happy. I feel more towards him than anyone else in the world. I wish he would just vanish and I'd never have to remember anything about him.

When I was born, the world was already full of Joona. He had golden hair, a bright voice, and a racing car covered with stickers, which he crashed over and over into the yellow painted wall of our room. One day the paint cracked into flaky figures and father locked the car in the attic.

Joona played sad songs on his brown plastic recorder and sat for hours with a picture book in front of him without turning the pages or saying a word. He dreamed of dropping me along with carrots, turnip cubes, and celery stalks into Grandma's old iron pot and stirring my pink baby flesh into a savoury stew. On bad days he crept over to my white crib and pulled my downy hair out of my head with both hands. On good days he pulled a blanket over the table in our room and we crawled under it to play. We had a torch and mashed banana and played Jonah in the belly of the whale. Joona pulled me into his lap and rocked me back and forth. I imagined behind the blanket a stormy sea, on whose waves our whale would rock up and down for ever.

Joona's golden hair and ringing voice are my first memories of the world. For a long time I was sure that Joona was the whole world.

On my plate there is a half-eaten mocha square and a ring of coffee left by my cup. The man at the table next to me stares into space and a tram clanks by outside the window. I close the book and run my fingers over its rough cover. I feel like apologizing to the people in the book.

5

When I was five and Joona seven, Father drove into our yard in an old hearse.

We were swinging with my mother. Joona sat alone on one swing and she held me in her lap on the other. When we heard the car horn, all three of us jumped up and ran to see what was happening. The car was big and black. The radiator grille had a big dent in it and someone had drawn a huge peepee in the dirt on a back window. I hoped my mother and father wouldn't see it. I tried to look like I didn't notice anything.

Father ran his fingers along the steering wheel. He had rolled the window down and *Roadrunner* was playing on the radio. His hair was messed up in the back, he had unbuttoned his top shirt buttons and golden chest hairs curled up out of the opening. He drummed on the wheel with his knuckles to the beat of the music and smiled so wide his teeth showed. My mother's hand was hard and tight around mine.

'Henri,' she said. She sounded as if she had to make an

effort to control her voice. Father closed his eyes and lifted a finger to his lips.

'Please don't.'

'We agreed.'

Father turned the music up and got out of the car. He smelled like he'd been at sea. He came up to us and lifted Joona and me in the air. My stomach flipped over.

'Let's go for a ride,' he said. 'A spring outing.'

Father pulled Mother close and I got squished in between. Father smelled of sweat and pipe tobacco and Mother of grass and her pink face lotion. Their smells mingled and plunged into me till I felt dizzy.

'Have dead people driven in that?' Joona asked. Father said they had. 'But they'll be happy to see a smiling boy in the back seat.' My mother didn't say anything. She turned away and I cried out, because at that moment I thought she would never come back. But when after a while she returned, she had put on a flowery Marimekko scarf and on her arm she carried a basket she'd bought at the market. In the basket were a bottle of juice, a packet of biscuits, and sandwiches wrapped in grease-proof paper. We climbed in the car, all four of us, Mother in the front seat next to Father and Joona and I in the back. The car's leather seats were hot from the sun and stuck to the backs of our legs.

'Maybe there's dead spirits in here,' Joona whispered. I thought of wrinkled old grandmas and grandpas sitting on the seat with us, nodding their tiny shrunken heads and eyeing the other cars for more dead people. The sun shone in through every window and when Joona sat in just the right spot, the peepee on the back window thrust up out of his head like a horn. Mother laid her hand on Father's thigh and I could see in the rear-view mirror how they both smiled a little. I turned around and knelt on the seat and waved at the bearded man in the car behind us, and laughed when the seat back hummed against my stomach.

We're a happy family, I thought. It felt like the sentence had flown into my mind from the page of a book. I imagined myself a rosy-cheeked pigtailed girl from a children's book, off on a huge exciting adventure for which someone had already written a happy ending.

Father drove fast. The front windows were open and an earthy wind blew my hair into my eyes. Mother clung to the hem of her scarf. Father honked his horn as he passed a Volkswagen beetle. The driver showed us his middle finger. Joona responded by making a circle with his thumb and forefinger and pumping his other forefinger through it. I stuck my thumbs in my ears and made a raspberry with my tongue.

'Henri,' Mother said quietly when Father passed a carrot-coloured Lada and two other cars. I saw her hand squeezing Father's thigh so hard her fingers were white. Father put his hand over Mother's and laughed.

'Ain't it great, kids?' he shouted over his shoulder. We mumbled something, because we didn't want them to get cross.

'*Vad i helvete menar du*?' Mother asked when Father passed a speeding sports car with its windows open and a motorcyclist wearing a leather jumpsuit: What the hell do you think you're doing? Mother always spoke Swedish when she didn't want us to understand. My stomach twisted and my skin got goosebumps, even though it was hot. I tried to take Joona's hand, but he had his clenched in fists and was staring at the back of Father's neck with a face as blank as a doll's.

'I'm enjoying life!' he shouted as if my mother were a long way away. 'You should try it some time. Just once!'

Then Father shouted: 'Shit!'

Glass tinkled.

Mother screamed.

Something went crunch. As if someone had broken a small bird's neck.

I was on the floor listening to a banging noise coming up out of the car. The carpet smelled like wet dog. Joona

12

breathed warm air onto the back of my neck. I scrunched my eyes shut and waited for someone to come and lift us out.

Mother was taken to the hospital in an ambulance. Father said it wasn't serious. His shirt front was splotched with blood from her nose. At the top, where the shirt was open, the blood had dyed his chest hairs into reddish-brown clumps.

When the ambulance men helped Mother into the ambulance, he didn't say anything. I sat on the curb and wrapped my arms around my knees. I didn't say anything either. Or else I was screaming. I can't really remember.

'Mother was just in shock,' Father said. 'When she comes back, everything will be like before. She will probably look funny with her nose all bandaged up. But otherwise everything will be fine. Just like before.'

We were sitting at the kitchen table and Father was grilling hot sandwiches. Joona knelt on the chair on his hands and stared at the wall. He hadn't said a word all evening. Father set the steaming sandwiches in front of us. Ham, pineapple, melted cheese. When Joona picked up his knife to cut into his sandwich, Father grabbed his hand.

'Let us pray,' he said. 'Let us thank the good Lord for watching over us today.'

The chair banged on the floor as Joona jerked his hand away and jumped up from the table. His cheeks were red and he looked at Father as if not really seeing him.

'What if it wasn't God?' Joona asked in a grown-up voice. 'What if it was the devil going into you and driving like crazy?'

'What?' Father said. Red splotches appeared on his neck. 'What did you say?'

The radio beeped to signal the hour. A piece of paint the shape of a face had flaked off the wall. I took a bite of hot cheese. Tears popped into my eyes. I held the glass of milk with both hands and drank. The milk ran cool into my mouth and all the way down to my stomach. It felt as if it were washing me clean on the inside. Washing me away.

6

Ian's father went crazy in the Vietnam War.

It had been almost a year since the Virginia Woolf lecture. We were sitting in a bar near the university. Along with the beer mugs we had pens, notepads, and messy scraps of paper on the table in front of us. Ian looked even more bent-over than before.

After the lecture Ian had gone back to New York and lived for a year in a tiny studio apartment with pigeons sleeping outside his window. Every morning he drank a cup of unsweetened espresso, jogged to the university and talked to students about literary theory and creative writing. In the evening he bought an Indian take-away, opened his laptop, and worked on his dissertation. The lights of Manhattan flickered on outside his windows, but Ian sat in a woollen sweater at the desk he had inherited from his grandfather and pondered when Western literature had begun to reflect a concept of humans as unique individuals.

In the autumn Ian got a cold. He stayed at home for a few days and worked on his dissertation from morning till night, slippers on his feet and a dusty blanket around his shoulders.

On the third morning of his cold his phone rang. On the other end was a history teacher from the university. 'Are you OK?' the caller asked. Ian thought he meant the cold.

When Ian realized what his friend meant, he couldn't say anything at all. He made a pot of coffee, wrapped his blanket around his neck like a shawl, and turned on the TV. Over and over again they showed the image of the plane crashing into the tall tower and the solid building crumbling into boulders and dust. At some point they showed the title: *America at War*.

'I kept thinking that I needed to do something. I imagined a lecture series on relations between the United States and the Middle Eastern countries, volunteer rescue work, or an article on the history of Afghanistan. But all I could do was watch TV. Then your university called and offered me this scholar exchange. I packed immediately.'

Ian looked at the drunken ponytail boys, who a moment before had been grilling him on why his homeland had bombed one of the world's poorest countries back to the Stone Age. He looked at me and a friend of mine, who were sitting across from him with our notepads saying nothing.

It was the first meeting of Ian's creative writing course.

My friend and I had come to the class because we longed for some change in our vague humanities-student lives. I had come because I wanted to hear Ian's voice again. I wanted Ian to read my poems about Joona, suffering, and death and find new meaning in them. I wanted him to find something in me.

Ian gave us an assignment. 'Write a poem and a short story about the worst thing that ever happened to you. Any approach.' He looked at me. I had been hoping he would. Then he told us about his father, and the war he'd fought in when he was younger than we were.

Where Ian was born, everyone went to church. The women curled their hair with rollers and the men cut theirs so short their scalps shone through at the temples. The streets in town were straight and wide and the locals drove big new cars; the Mexicans from across the border drove smaller and older ones. When minors committed crimes, their parents paid fines or went to jail. The rich houses were surrounded by high walls, the lawns were even, and the gardens looked like they were out of a magazine. The shops sold soap and toilet paper in giant-sized packages, and the streets were perpetually, ominously quiet.

Ian wasn't supposed to be born. His mother and father weren't supposed to get together.

She was the cleverest girl in her high school; she published essays and short stories in the school paper. He was a good-looking but not particularly bright boy, with full lips, and hips that swayed when he danced. It was a spring evening. There was rum swiped from his father's liquor cabinet, her minidress, his pink sports car.

Because that night was never supposed to be, Ian's parents packed up and moved to New York. His mother hid her pregnancy and got into college. His father did odd jobs in construction and the restaurant business and waited for something to happen. His mother slept next to his father but smiled most freely with a whole other class of people. People who read books and talked all night. His father didn't smile anywhere. He caressed Ian's mother's thin back and swollen breasts and dreamed of a revolution or a war that would give him a chance to show what he was made of.

When Ian was four, the United States started to move troops into Vietnam. Ian's mother wore Indian cotton dresses and wooden bead jewellery. His father drove a cab and in the evenings pumped iron. On his mother's way to the university in the morning, she dressed Ian warmly and took him to the building across the street to be taken care of by a black woman.

'I doubt there was anything political about it,' Ian told me when I asked why his father wanted to go to war. 'He probably had no idea what communism meant. Or where Vietnam was. It was mostly just frustration. Or a vague longing for meaning.'

Ian leaned back and lit his pipe. Sucked his cheeks in and half-closed his eyes. The smoke rose in blue swirls towards the ceiling. 'After the war had been on for a while, she took me to a demonstration. It's my first clear memory.'

Ian had never seen so many people in the same place. He swayed back and forth in the backpack with elephants on it and looked over his mother's shoulder at the sea of people that surged chaotically in all directions. Almost everyone had long hair, the men too. Ian's mother had tied a silk fringe scarf around her forehead. Ian played with the knot on the back of her neck, and when he accidentally pulled her hair she slapped him on the thigh. He cried.

His mother danced in place to calm him down, and next to them a man with braids played a tambourine and moved his hips. Over the sea of people rose gigantic sheets with PEACE painted on them in many colours. Someone somewhere was shouting raspily into a megaphone. Every now and then people would shout something in unison. Ian wrapped his arms around his mother's neck and felt the movement and warmth of her back against his chest. His stomach ached. For some reason it seemed as though his mother could slip out of the backpack at any moment, drop Ian on the street, and run away.

When his father came back from the war, Ian no longer went to the black woman's place during the day. He went to school and sat at home in the afternoons reading books. He had thick glasses and a skinny body and on the first day of school some sixth-grade boys shoved his head in the toilet. Ian never told his mother about that. He also never told her when some boys from another class stole his shoes and socks and locked him in a toilet stall during break and peed under the door onto his bare feet. Ian was late to class and got detention. At home his mother ruffled his hair and asked whether something was wrong. Ian said no and believed it himself.

His mother bought books at the university and in second-hand bookshops, and Ian devoured every one, cover to cover. It felt to him that as long as he could immerse himself in new stories every afternoon and evening, it wouldn't matter what happened to him in his own life, he'd be OK. He'd be fine with a stomach ache every morning, and the trips to school when someone would creep up behind him and throw rocks at his back. The playtimes when no-one would talk to him. The school corridors and dark corners, where someone would lie in ambush for him, pop out and bang his head against a coat rack. The regular disappearances of his backpack and glasses and their reappearance either broken or stinking of urine or scribbled on with a black marker.

Ian was sure that, as long as he could forget that he was a small boy who had to wake up and go to school, he could take anything: the quiet evenings and nights when he couldn't sleep or when his mother came home in the small hours giggling and smelling of something sweet. With books he was sure he could stand anything, anything at all that happened to him.

Then came a day when Ian came home from school to find a strange man sitting across from his mother at the kitchen table. They were talking in low voices and now and then awkwardly holding hands. The man was bent over. His hair was grey, his teeth were brown, his eyes were bloodshot. When Ian dropped his backpack by the kitchen door, the man and his mother stopped talking.

'Honey,' his mother said too loudly, 'come say hello to your father.' The man didn't stick out his hand. Ian let his own hand hang uncertainly in the air for a moment, then patted the man on the shoulder. 'Hi.' The man jumped at his touch. His lips moved in time with Ian's. His mother took Ian's hand. 'Your father has had a hard time,' she said as if to a small child. 'He may be a bit different from how he was before.' Ian nodded. He poured himself a glass of milk and sat for a while at the table with his mother and father. 'I'm going to go and read,' he said finally. 'You guys can talk in peace.'

Ian turned the pages. He saw the letters, the words and sentences, but couldn't enter the book's world. He read on, followed the plot and the characters' thoughts. But the whole time he knew that he was a small boy who no-one talked to at school. He knew that on the other side of the wall sat his mother, who was acting strange, and a man who didn't remember he was his father.

Ian looked out of the window. People walking with umbrellas, streetlamps glowing pink, shiny yellow taxis. He felt like opening the window, standing up on the sill, and pushing off hard into the dark.

He sat there until evening, turning the pages. In the kitchen his father's deep voice mingled with his mother's high one. When the streetlamps had turned a foggy white and the sky an ominous black, his mother came in and put her hand on his shoulder. 'I put your father in your bed. You can sleep with me for a while. OK?'

I promised Ian I'd write about my own father next time. I just didn't know what had happened to him. I still don't know what it was.

7

We were in the kitchen and I was drinking milk. Father sat at the table with his mouth open and Joona stood next to him with his hair messed up.

'What did you say?' Father asked. 'What the hell did you just say?'

'Maybe it was the devil,' Joona repeated. 'The devil, devil, devil. The devil came up from hell and slid into you.' Through the bottom of the glass I could see a horned head. I swallowed, even though I didn't have anything in my mouth. Father stood up. Joona's head barely came up to his chest. They glared at each other. I held my breath.

'Come here,' Father said. Joona did not move. Father took a step forward. The floor creaked. Joona stared at Father without blinking. Father grabbed Joona by the hair. Joona's ears went red, but he still said nothing. My lungs hurt.

'You will never talk to me like that again. Do you understand?'

'You could have killed Mother,' Joona said. 'You could have killed all of us.'

Father pulled so hard on Joona's hair that he had to bend his head. I blew on the hot sandwich. Joona dropped to his knees on the floor. Father kept his hand at the back of Joona's neck and pressed his face against the floor. I closed my eyes.

'Dear God,' I said in my mind, the way Father had taught us to pray. 'Don't let anything bad happen. Don't let anything bad, anything bad, anything bad. Dear dear God don't let anything bad anything bad anything bad God anything bad anything bad dear dear dear dear God dear God don't.'

The sound of cloth tearing. The sound of Father's panting. No sound of Joona breathing at all.

I kept my eyes closed and called to God. Father had taught us that God sees everything. He hears when you call him. He comes when you need him. Ask and you shall receive. Seek and you shall find. Knock and the door will be open unto you. I remembered the song from Sunday school, and being unsure what door we were singing about. Father had played the squeaky harmonium with shoulders bent, and I had imagined myself pounding on a huge iron door with my fist, and a long-haired god shuffling over to open it in his white bathrobe and floor-slapping slippers.

I was behind that door again. 'Open, God,' I shouted in

my mind so loud that my throat hurt. Tears burned hot behind my eyelids and I squeezed my clasped hands tightly under my thighs. 'Dear God please open please!'

I heard a loud slap. Then another, a third, a fourth.

Father's breath came in harsh gasps. Joona whimpered. My stomach felt as though it was on fire. Joona didn't sound like a child, more like an animal caught in a trap. I opened my eyes.

Joona lay on the floor in the fetal position. His shirt was torn in two across the back and he had covered his face with his hands. The individual bumps of his spine poked his skin up like a dragon's fin. My Joona was a dragon child. I wished his skin had been a dragon's skin, thick scaly leather.

It wasn't. The skin on Joona's back had been fair, smooth child's skin, with a little peach fuzz. Now it was striped with wide red welts.

Father had wrapped the buckle end of his belt around his hand. He leaned against the table with his other hand, his hair was matted against his temples and his forehead glittered with sweat. Without a belt his trousers hung loosely on his hips. Under them I could see the wrinkled elastic band of his underpants and the golden hairs under his bellybutton. Joona was no longer whimpering. He was muttering something, over and over. It took me a while to realize that he was saying 'devil'. Father figured that out at the same time.

25

'Shut up goddammit!' Father shouted. The leather belt slapped against Joona's bare back between the torn halves of the shirt.

Shut up! Shut up! Shut up!

Devil. Devil. Devil.

Slap! Slap! Slap!

'Father please don't! Faaaaaather! Faaaaaaaaaaaaaather!'

That was me. I hung off Father's wrist with both hands. Snot and tears ran down my face and in through the neck of my blouse.

Father dropped his hand. He had wrapped the belt around his palm so tightly that the flesh bulged whitely around it on both sides. He wiped sweat from his brow and looked at me. Then he looked at Joona. Joona had stopped muttering. The welts on his back oozed blood.

Father looked at the belt and his floppy trousers. He looked back and forth from Joona to me, as if trying to remember who we were and how we had all got there. He pulled his belt back through his belt-loops and ruffled my hair. 'OK,' he said quietly. 'OK now. OK. OK.'

Father turned, drank some water straight from the tap, and walked out of the room. The front door banged. The clock's second hand clicked.

I sat next to Joona and took his head in my lap. His

hair smelled of sweat and vanilla shampoo. I ran my fingers slowly across his scalp. I had climbed up onto Mother's dressing table that morning and painted my nails brownish-red. The nails looked like shining drops of blood in Joona's hair, the fingers like wrinkled pink worms. Joona's breathing evened out.

'Please take this away,' I called to God and imagined myself caressing Joona's thoughts through his skin. 'Take all of this away and let everything be like before. Dear dear God. Please let everything be like before.' Joona's torn shirt flapped open on both sides of his ribs and the drops of blood on his back dried into scabs. 'I'll do whatever you ask,' I promised God. 'I'll clean our room every day. I'll help Mother. I'll go to bed on time. I'll give my allowance to the children in Africa. When I grow up I'll become a nun and move to India. If you take all this away, I'll never ask for anything ever again and I'll just do everything you want.'

I'm not sure how long we were on the floor like that, neither of us saying anything, Joona's head in my lap. I was positive that time had stopped or changed somehow. I was positive that something in the whole world had irrevocably changed.

Finally Joona got up. He still didn't say anything, but let me help him to bed. His hand was thin and feverishly warm.

It filled my hand completely, my fingers wouldn't go around it. I squeezed it as hard as I could. Joona squeezed lightly back. I looked straight ahead. I didn't want to see his back any more.

When Joona was a baby and I wasn't born yet, Mother and Father painted the walls in the children's room yellow as the sun. They painted a row of winking sunflowers around the tops of the walls and bought a yellow towelling bedspread for his crib.

'Children need sun,' Mother had said. Father had set the paint roller in the tray, come to Mother and put his arm around her waist. Maybe they kissed. Maybe they made love right then, their shirts and arms speckled with yellow paint. Maybe they made me that day. Maybe after making love they lay there on the floor, Mother's head on Father's chest. Maybe they dreamed of the years to come. I think they closed their eyes and saw the same pictures at the same time.

The yellow room is bathed in sun. It's Saturday and the sheets have just been changed on the yellow-painted beds.

The room smells of fabric softener and children's soap. Two children, a girl and a boy, sit side by side on the bed. The boy reads the girl a book. On the bedside table is a serving tray with a heart design, on it two glasses of milk and two buns fresh from the oven. A man and a woman, father and mother, stand in the doorway with their arms around each other. They are going on an outing and the picnic basket is packed. Outside the windows the birches are budding and the raspy sound of a radio carries to them from somewhere. The man and woman smile at each other. The children raise their eyes from the book and smile at them.

'Are we going already?' the boy asks, and the man picks him up. The woman puts the bonnet she crocheted herself on the girl's head. They walk out hand in hand, all four. The basket is on the mother's arm. The father carries the car keys. Everywhere is the smell of life and spring. They go out and spend a wonderful day together. It passes quickly, but this doesn't bother them. The man and the woman know that there are many more such wonderful days ahead than either of them can count.

I was five and Joona seven. I helped Joona into our yellow room and pulled back the yellow towelling bedspread.

'You should sleep,' I said. 'Everything will be better in the morning.'

Joona sat on the bed and let me pull his torn shirt off. I stuffed it deep into the wastebasket, under the empty juice cartons, the wads of gum, the pieces of paper. When Joona climbed under the blanket, I sat next to him and let my fingers walk across his scalp, the back of his neck, his arms.

Finally Joona fell asleep. I climbed up on the plastic stool and turned off the light. The red nightlight glowed from the corner of the bed like a red eye.

I was almost out of the room when I heard Joona whispering behind me. 'I'll kill him,' he said, so quietly that at first I thought I'd heard him wrong. 'I'm gonna kill Dad some day.'

It took a moment before the weight of the words hit me.

But by the time I was out of the door, and saw my moonlit reflection in the hall mirror, I understood. It would be my job to make sure that the day's shadows would fade away and all our lives would have a happy ending.

Night came, the dark settled in, but father did not come home. I lay in bed with my eyes open and did not fall asleep even when I heard Joona's even breathing from across the room. I crushed Joona's old stuffed dog against my chest and tried to make the pain inside me go away. 'I'll do anything,' I repeated. 'Anything, if you take this day out of our lives.'

I woke in the morning having to pee. I had fallen asleep with my clothes on and my teeth unbrushed. They felt rough against my tongue. I tried to creep quietly to the bathroom so I wouldn't wake Joona. The kitchen door was open a crack and a dim light glowed through. I tiptoed to the crack and saw Father's wide, bent-over back. He sat at the table with no shirt on and his face resting on his hands. Beside him were a glass, and a half-full whisky bottle. 'Father,' I whispered, but he didn't seem to hear. I walked to him and put my hand on his shoulder. His skin was sticky.

Father turned. His breath smelled. He took my hand and looked at me long and hard, as if I were a strange lost child and he needed to decide what to do with me.

'Father,' I whispered again. 'Father.'

Father lifted me into his lap. He pressed my head against his chest so hard that it was hard for me to breathe. He wrapped his arms tightly around me, pressed his face into my hair and rocked my upper body slowly back and forth.

That had been my safe place. Father had always lifted me into his lap when I was sad or afraid. I had rocked with my head against his chest the previous autumn, after my first day in kindergarten.

Joona had been teased in nursery school, and I was afraid the same would happen to me. So I made sandcakes by myself over in the corner of the yard and watched the other children pushing each other on the swings. Then when we sat down to eat after playing outside, something horrible happened.

Suddenly my bottom was warm and wet and the boy next to me shouted loudly, 'Eww, yuck, Anna peed her pants!'

A teacher's assistant with hard fingers carried me by the armpits to the bathroom, stripped off my wet tights and dropped them on the floor, then lifted me onto the edge of the toilet. Up above there was a mirror and I could see my white face, my chubby thighs glistening with drops of pee, and behind them the assistant's tight lips. 'The only children who wet their pants here are the handicapped ones,' she said and splashed scalding hot water on my bottom. I squinched my own lips tight to keep from crying. I counted to ten over and over in my head. I knew that if I only counted enough times, Father would come and take me away.

That evening I cried hot trembling tears and Father held me in his lap till I fell asleep. That happened on many other days and evenings too, when I fell on my bike and scraped my knee or when the neighbouring girls wouldn't play with me. On days like that I curled up in Father's arms and knew that with his arms around me nothing evil could ever enter my world.

Now evil had crept into Father's lap, and I would never again have a safe place to flee.

I held my breath. Father's chest moved against my cheek.

I squeezed my eyes shut and decided to travel far away, to fly out through the narrow opening of the window and climb high up the hill of the lightening night sky.

Father was trembling. Hot tears flowed out of his eyes into my hair, but I was already gone. I shot out over the city on the spring wind, over the backyard, the kindergarten and Joona's school, over the church, where Father had held the funeral service for the single woman next door that day. I flew over the ice-cream kiosk to the seashore and rode the waves to places I didn't even know existed.

Behind my eyelids I saw spots in glowing colours and knew that somewhere far away there lived a little girl who sat on her weeping father's lap in the morning and was so afraid that she wanted to die.

8

'But why did your father act like that?'

It was a February evening and we were walking on the ice. The wind whirled snow up into clouds around us and we pulled our scarves tight around our faces. Behind us glowed the lights of the city, above us the dim light of the stars and the purplish-red sky. Ian squeezed my hand through my mitten.

Ian had read my short story. I had sat quietly outside his office, pressing my fists to my eyes and listening to the blood rushing through my head. Please let him like it, I'd repeated to myself.

Please let him like it.

I'd nodded to the professor walking by with his glasses in his hand. I'd talked about movies with the boy who was working in the library instead of serving in the army. I'd torn my chapped lip and spilled coffee on my skirt.

Please let him like it.

Please let him like it.

Please let him like me.

Finally Ian opened the door. The story hung from his hand. He looked at me for so long that I wanted to disappear. 'Are you busy?' he asked. 'I thought we could talk about it a little.'

We walked down the stairs and out into the snow. We walked down a snowy hill to the market square, around which old-fashioned streetlamps burned. We walked along icy streets past stuccoed houses, tiny bars, and delis only open during the day. We crossed the long bridge over the booming ice, with the lights from the hotel gleaming on its surface. The people huddled at the bus stop shielded their faces against the wind, small boys ran red-eared across the market square, and the pigeons on the eaves of the old market hall slept like stones.

Out on the ice Ian took my hand.

We walked along side by side, almost pressed up against each other. We talked less, walked more slowly than before. It was bitterly cold, and we had to hunch over against the wind. My coat was too thin and snow blew in on my wrists. I balled my fists inside my mittens. Ian was on my right. His coat sleeve touched mine.

My right arm was completely warm. We did not stop or look at each other. We said nothing. I don't remember opening my fist. But all of a sudden his hand was around mine, and that was all I knew.

'But why did your father act like that?'

Ian's voice came to me muffled and dim through my scarf. He squeezed my hand and I squeezed back. We were out on the ice far from the shore, the snow barked under our steps and whipped up on the wind so that sometimes we could see nothing.

Why did my father act like that? Should I have known? Should someone? Was he my father then?

Was he the same father who made toasted sandwiches, built a tent in the living room, and rocked away the world's woes in his lap? The same father from the picture in Joona's baby book, holding his tiny son in his arms before I even existed? The father who stood by our beds at night singing 'Lullaby, and goodnight,' and pressed his forehead against the windowpane when he thought we were already asleep?

I don't know. I hardly know my father at all.

He never talked about himself. He listened, he asked what Joona and Mother and I thought about things. But he himself never talked about anything but music, cars, and who he had married or buried. If we asked, he talked about God. He talked about a loving father who forgave us our sins and protected us from evil.

As a child I prayed every night that God would take care of my father.

Even though Father would never talk about himself, Gran would sometimes tell us bits and pieces of stories about her son. She'd sit in her little kitchenette on a red kitchen stool peeling potatoes and remember the times when my father was a small boy and she herself a quiet woman who looked older than she was.

I would sit on a stool at Gran's feet peeling carrots. Making a stew. In the winter we made meat stew and in the summer we made fish stew, for which we bought fish fresh from the market, from a bearded fisherman. As he walked away the man winked at Gran. I hoped they'd get married. I hoped that Gran would get to walk down the aisle on the fisherman's arm in a white gown and with a crown woven of rowan branches on her head. I'd stand next to the altar and hand over a ring glittering with diamonds and a sea-blue stone in the middle.

'Don't be silly,' Gran said when I told her my dream. 'I've always been a one-man woman.'

'What, are you saying you and Gramp were happy?'

Gran didn't answer.

Maybe she was, before Father was born. Before the war.

Maybe she was happy when Gramp came knocking on her window in the wee hours one morning and took her rowing on a misty lake. Maybe she was happy-sad when she saw Gramp off at the train station as the war began. They had just been married and Gramp promised to love her for ever. Gran gripped his collar with both hands and the smokestack on the locomotive let loose a stream of smoke.

When the war was over, Gran walked in the market square with flowers in her arms and knew that the fear was over and the men would be home soon. She pressed her face into the flowers and thought about her husband's hair.

The man who returned from the front was exhausted and almost unrecognizable. He sat hunched over at the long table and wordlessly drank himself into a stupor.

Most evenings he toppled off the bench onto the floor and Gran had to drag him to bed by the armpits. Sometimes he would pull her next to him, breathe his boozy breath on her and pull her skirt up with cold hands. A year after the war ended, out on the sauna bench she gave birth to a wrinkly boy.

'Your pa was so sweet,' she said. Her eyes misted over. 'He was so sweet and helped with everything, and even when he was little he'd run to defend me when his pa was in one of his moods. I thank the good Lord for taking care of him. For letting him grow up to be a man and have a family of his own.'

*

We walked on the ice and Ian wanted to know about my father. What on earth could I say?

Should I tell him Gran's story about the boy who stood in the corner with an axe and listened to his mother crying and his father breaking down the door? Should I have drawn him a picture of a small village on Christmas Eve, the starry sky and beneath it the house whose windows ring with the sound of the door opening?

Out of the door runs an eight-year-old boy.

The boy's hair is tousled from sleep, his bare skin steaming in the cold, the wing bones on his thin back like the stumps of actual wings. The boy runs barefoot in the snow and the man who appears in the doorway holds the jamb and shouts: 'Look at that Henri go! What a runner!' The boy runs on, his feet bare, his hands clenched in fists. The neighbours' curtains quiver, the man goes back inside, and the boy runs on, fists clenched, until he falls face first into the snow. He lies there, cheek on snow, until his mother finds him, wraps him in a blanket, and carries him to a neighbour's front hall to sleep.

That's my image of Father, and thinking about it always hurts in the same place.

Should I have drawn Ian that picture and said look, here's our story, here's where it all started? I wanted to. I wanted to find that place. Make a keyhole to peek through at life. Gramp, Gran, Father, Mother, Joona, me. Our story's beginning. But you don't tell other people things like that. You imagine them all by yourself, in secret, while waiting for sleep or a bus. And the next moment you re-imagine the whole thing, differently.

'Why did your father act like that?'

Ian was squeezing my hand and though I had been dreaming about that for a long time I pulled my hand away.

'How the hell should I know?' I stepped away from him, pushed my hands in my pockets and walked so fast that I left him behind.

'Anna,' he said quietly, grabbing the flapping end of my scarf. 'I'm sorry.'

He stood in front of me.

There was snow on his coat.

He wrapped his arms around me and my ski cap fell to the ground.

Ian's mouth tasted of coffee and peppermint gum and his stubble scraped my skin. The blowing snow hid us inside it. Ian pulled me tightly against his rough sweater.

9

When Ian's father came back from the war he began to have nightmares.

His father slept in Ian's bed and Ian tried to sleep next to his mother. Most nights he couldn't sleep. He lay there awake listening to his father screaming in the next room. When his mother woke, got up, and went to stroke his father's brow, Ian pretended to be asleep. He pulled his blanket up over his head, squeezed his eyes shut tight, and began to tell himself a story about a different kind of father.

'In that story,' he said, 'Dad came back from the war and understood the meaning of life.'

We were sitting on my sofa, drinking wine. It was late and our legs were touching. The warmth of Ian's skin spread through denim to my skin and I wondered whether he felt the same thing and what he thought about it. Our wet clothes from our walk were draped over the radiator in the bathroom and my heart was beating too hard. Ian's head slid down onto my shoulder.

'In my story Dad bought a motorbike and a black leather coverall and took off driving across the continent.' Ian's eyes were half closed. I looked at the lines that circled his eyes like a superthin spiderweb, and thought about his life before I was born. I saw a little boy under his blanket in the dark. I wanted to hug that little boy.

In Ian's story his father rode his motorbike all over America and built houses for the people who were damaged by the war. The people painted their houses with bright colours and planted fruit trees in the back gardens. The houses had swimming pools and doctors and clubs where people played the guitar and drew pictures.

Ian began to tell this story to himself every evening. His father gradually became a superhero who could walk through walls and see the future and read people's thoughts. He souped up his motorbike so that he could ride it in the water and in the air, and finally under the earth and into outer space.

When the boys in his class shot spitwads at Ian or jostled him in the halls between classes, he closed his eyes and thought of the evening to come, when he would curl up under his blanket and head off with his superhero father on new adventures. On weekends, when his mother and father would sit across the table from each other without saying a word and no-one would call him up and ask him out to play,

Ian took the metro to the library and devoured books on geography and astronomy, looking for new settings for his story, ancient cities, canyons plunging to great depths, or uncharted planets, to which his father could travel on his go-anywhere motorbike.

Ian no longer minded the mornings when his mother's hand shook and the cereal spilled onto the floor, or the nights when his father's screams split the air.

He was so focused on his new father that he didn't notice how his real father's nightmares began to torment him during the day as well, and how his mother forgot to pay the electricity bill or sweep up the cereal that fell on the floor.

On the day when Ian came home from school and found his mother sitting at the kitchen table in a bathrobe with a strange man's hand on her thigh, he had peach fuzz on his upper lip.

His mother's eyelids were red and she had a piece of tomato skin between her teeth. For the first time he noticed how old she looked. He sat down across from his mother and stuck out his hand to the strange man. The man had long hair and was wearing a corduroy jacket with a scarf around his neck.

'Michael's an old friend,' his mother said. 'He came over to help out a little.'

The man shook Ian's hand. His grip was like what you'd use to grab a runaway horse or an underwater handful of hair. Ian looked the man in the eye.

'What's going on?'

'Your father's been taken in for treatment,' the man explained. 'He's fine. He's in a special hospital for post-traumatic stress disorder. They're hoping to medicate his hallucinations. I'll be helping your mom out for a while. She's had it tough. I guess you've noticed.'

He hadn't. He felt shame. It felt to him as if his mother and father had been shipwrecked and he himself had swum ashore and had become so absorbed collecting corals that he'd forgotten all about them. But he noticed that the strange man looked lovingly at his mother, though her hair was greasy and her teeth were dirty. Ian smiled at the man.

'Everything's gonna be fine,' the man said.

Ian nodded, patted his mother's hand, and went into his own room.

He looked at himself in the mirror. He had slimmed down and grown taller. His hands and feet seemed bigger than before, almost too big for the rest of his body. There were three red pimples on his chin and black spots on his nose. He got goosebumps. He had no idea who he was.

Ian pulled off his sweater. He had hair in his armpits. He

raised one arm, put his nose down there, and sniffed. He smelled different, stronger, tangier. Almost like the men paving the night-time streets, who shouted over the noise of the engines about women and fucking, and whose arms glistened with sweat. Almost like his father, when Ian was small.

Ian locked his door and undid his belt. He dropped his jeans and underpants and looked down. His penis had changed. It had become bigger and darker and it had fine hairs growing around it. He touched it cautiously. It quivered. He trembled.

He closed his eyes and listened to the rushing of his blood. It truly rushed. There was a murmuring throughout his body, something he'd never noticed before. Everything had happened without his noticing, while he was off in his imaginary world. Now he was here. He looked at his long legs and arms, his dark nipples and penis, which hung between his legs startlingly, as if someone had sneaked in and secretly fixed it there. He looked at the alien body in the mirror and decided that he would have to do something about it.

He got a job.

Three times a week after school he walked to the supermarket and packed people's groceries into shiny plastic bags. He wore a red cap and a striped shirt with his name on his breast pocket. Before he went to work he had to clean under his nails and polish his shoes.

At the cash register sat a woman ten years older than Ian who had red painted nails. He could see flashes of her bra between the buttons of her blouse. When their eyes met, the woman winked at him.

At the end of every month Ian counted the money he had made. He wrote the total in a notebook that he carried with him everywhere. Besides his wages, he jotted down things he overheard in the metro, or saw on the street or in the supermarket. Things like: *An old man let the pigeons eat from his mouth.* Or: *A woman came into the store wearing only one shoe. Why?* Or: *On my lunch hour a clean-looking man sat across from me who had a yellowish bruise under his eye. Did his suit hide even bigger bruises?*

After his father moved out and Michael moved in, Ian's mother started washing her hair again, and using lipstick, and wearing jeans that made her legs look like a young woman's. Ian was happy to see his mother humming in the kitchen in the morning and not dumping cereal on the floor. But he was also sad for his father.

His father lived in a tiny room in a veterans' nursing home and took medications that slurred his speech and dulled his eyes. The things he said made no sense, and he looked old enough to be Ian's grandfather. After every visit to his father

Ian walked for hours on unfamiliar streets, stopped on bridges to stare at the river, and fished in his pockets for small coins to throw into the water.

Ian saved his wages to get his father out of the veterans' home.

He saved most of every pay-packet in order to buy a house in the country that his father could move to. His father could paint the walls and plant whatever he wanted in the garden. In the back there would be a workshop where he could build wooden boats or model planes. The planes would have real engines and they would fly them out in the meadow behind the house. Ian would live in the house with his father, write books, and call in a doctor whenever his father needed treatment.

Ian still told stories about his father every evening, but now he was himself the superhero, and his real father, the house in the country, the garden and the workshop, were part of the story.

He thought about the house, the workshop, and the garden every evening as he stood at the end of the conveyor belt packing strangers' groceries into plastic bags. He wanted the house so badly that it already seemed to be waiting for him.

Ian was even thinking of the house, the garden, and the workshop when the woman with the red nails stopped in the staff room beside him.

'What are you doing this evening?' she asked. She was so close to him that Ian could smell her scent, which consisted of sweat, sweet perfume, and peppermint gum. Something in it made Ian's groin swell and the hairs on his arms stand up on end. He fished around in his bag as long as he could.

'Nothing much,' he said. He took his deodorant and a clean shirt out of the bottom of his bag and forced himself to breathe deeply.

'I was just thinking,' the woman said, and bent over so that her breast bumped Ian's back, 'I'm going to the movies and was thinking maybe you'd like to come along?'

Ian breathed. No problem. Think before you open your mouth.

'Why not?' he said, and thought that his voice came out sounding almost grown-up. 'What are you going to see?'

On the screen was jungle. Bombs dropped into the green terrain, and with each explosion something tore inside him. A hypnotic male voice sang *This is the end, my only friend, the end*, and the jungle, the bombs, the bloody torn limbs and women's garish clothing rolled into Ian as if he were dreaming. He could feel the woman's arm near him. He felt dizzy.

He saw his own father in that jungle, torn apart by the power of the chaos churning around him, and finally letting it inside. He saw his father's eyes, dulled by drugs.

'I gotta go,' Ian whispered to the woman. 'I don't feel good.' She got up with him. They walked hunched over out in front of the other filmgoers, who coughed drily.

When they were out in the street, Ian vomited. He leaned against the wall with one hand and the woman held his long hair out of his face. The vomit had tomato sauce and pieces of spaghetti in it, and his whole body jerked with its passing. Every time Ian closed his eyes, the jungle spread out behind his eyelids. He had passed from the world into the film, into his father's mind or into a new reality, in which the images on the screen and the memories of all veterans blurred together and formed a web that he could not escape.

Ian could feel the woman's hand on the back of his neck. Her touch was soft and heavy. The woman had not wound up in the jungle. She wore a white blouse and jeans and a denim jacket, and she was thoroughly grounded in the world with ice-cream bars, yellow taxi cabs, coffee makers, and lunch meetings. In that world time passed as promised, people woke up in the morning and knew where to go. Doctors had clean white jackets and the sick were given tranquillizers. There were smiles and peaceful afternoons and moments in which

49

people touched each other half by accident and something happened between them.

The weight of the woman's hand drew Ian back into that world.

We'd finished our glasses of wine. Ian's head was in my lap and I ran my fingers through his hair. I wanted to reach through his scalp all the way to his thoughts. When I closed my eyes and focused on the roughness of his skin under my fingers, I imagined that I could.

'That was my first time,' Ian said.

I swallowed. I felt the thinning hair at his temples, the curve of his forehead and the birthmark behind his left ear. The dent at the back of his neck and the stubble on his cheeks, the acne scars under the stubble. The softness of his skin under his shirt. His breath coming faster as my hand moved down.

I saw that evening. Thin Ian and the stretched buttons on the woman's blouse. The jeans dropping in a pile on the frayed wall-to-wall carpet. The wandering of eyes as they searched for something appropriate to look at. The woman's glowing white skin. I saw it through Ian's eyes. The rounded surfaces, at once arousing and frightening, the abundant flesh that must must must be touched this instant. Timid exploratory fingers covered by a tender strong hand. Ian's lips, teeth, and tongue.

Ian's lips were dry and his tongue tasted of wine. His skin smelled of the cold, tobacco, and sweat. His hands were large, strong, and rough.

10

Mum,

I've gone out and don't know when I'll be back.

Dad tore my science notebook when we fought. Anna's trying to glue it with something.

Maybe I won't be back at all.

Joona
P.S. Don't worry. I've done my homework.

11

The hospital is next to the park.

In the ward my Joona is in, the hall door is always kept locked, but the bathroom doors must be kept open. The balcony is fenced in with wire mesh, and the people behind the mesh have eyes dulled by drugs, and tobacco stains on their fingertips. Through the mesh I can see a gridded landscape: the manicured paths through the park, the dense maples, the wooden benches, and the church from whose wooden steeple a young man jumped many years ago. The people standing on the balcony often speak of that young man. They speak of him dreamily – and of the other who jumped from a bridge and whose body got caught on the propeller of a sunken ship – as of a secret crush on a stranger who has looked at them just long enough.

In Joona's room there are four beds and next to the beds, eight slippers, each with the name of the hospital printed on it. On the day that I don't want to remember, Joona drank cleaning fluid from the cleaning lady's cart, had to have his stomach pumped, and then fled. It was winter and he ran through the city in his open bathrobe, bare feet in slippers. He ran through the city and his name was announced on the police radio. He ran as if there were some place to which he might go.

I should sit on the edge of Joona's bed, take his scarred hand in mine, and ask him how he's feeling. I should listen to his answer. Chat about this and that.

I should tell him that the sun is shining outside and when he's released I'll come to meet him and carry his bag. I'll take him to the shore for an ice cream and a beer in an outdoor café and on a bike ride wherever he wants to go. I'll be with him and tell people, See, this is my brother, and I love him so much that I won't let anyone think ill of him.

People talk about this hospital. 'Any more of this and they'll be taking me there,' they say, knowing that of course no-one will be taking them there. No-one thinks of this hospital as a place where you might spend weeks, months, or years. A place where you go to visit the person you love most in the world. The only people who speak out loud about this hospital are the ones who have never had anything to do with it.

I can't go there. I don't want to think about it.

I want to go to visit Joona in some tiny rented studio apartment somewhere far away, make a pot of coffee and tell him that Mother has been a pain again. I want us to get accidentally drunk and reminisce about our childhood. I want a childhood to reminisce about. A life to tell others about. A brother with a real life.

I sit down on a sun-warmed bench with my book in my lap and light a cigarette. I want this moment, nothing more. I want to be any woman on a sunny day on a park bench, waiting for someone or going somewhere. To read this book. I want to be in 1920s England, where a weary writer looks at a man and a woman disappearing into the street and feels lonely, feels the presence of the devil.

I want to sit on a sun-warmed bench with the scent of fresh-mown lawn beneath it and an arching maple above it. Read a book about the devil, read beautiful sentences and think that maybe I understand. Sit here, sniff the wind, and know that it'll be summer soon and the sea will be warm.

Two young girls walk along the gravel lane with their arms around each other's backs. They are a little younger than I was when Joona was taken to the hospital for the first time. The girls have thick-soled running shoes, baggy jeans, and tight shirts that show the hooks on their bra straps a little. At their age I hated my breasts. I hid them under a big fuzzy sweater and died of shame when the boys pushed their cool hands under my shirt. The girls smoke cigarettes with grown-up mannerisms and when they laugh their teeth flash white.

12

If you left the hospital and headed down towards the shore you'd come to the grounds of a second hospital. The second hospital's stone walls were carved with figures. A princess's castle, I thought when I was a girl, whenever we walked hand in hand into the building to talk about Joona.

I knew that Joona had *something*. Something that made him sit quiet for hours, and then suddenly, at home, in day care or school, raise his eyes and start talking about Satan. I saw it in his face at night, when he stood at the window alone, back bent, his wingbones making little tents in his pyjama top. At moments like that I squeezed my fingers till they turned red, and prayed that God would see my Joona and take care of him.

Mother explained that the someone in Joona made Father lose his temper. 'Henri's afraid,' Mother said after the car trip when I held the phone receiver in my hand and told her that I'd called the child protectors to come to take us away. 'He loves Joona, but doesn't know what to do.' She stroked my head as she hung up the phone and bent down to pull the plug out of the wall beneath the chest of drawers. 'They need help. We girls are stronger and we'll help them, won't we?'

'Yes.'

We girls sat in the family room at the children's hospital, in chairs arranged in a circle, next to Father and Joona. Across from our family sat two smiling women with notepads, and in the wall was a mirror that was a window, and behind that mirror that was a window sat a doctor. They all wanted to help us. Find out what was in Joona and how to get it out. I loved them all for that. And because they asked me to play house with little dolls and jotted down notes in their notepads.

'Prolonged period of negativism,' the women said after our car trip, when Father told them about Joona's devil talk. No word of what happened after that. 'Difficult puberty,' said other women in another room after Joona had been picked on so mercilessly in junior high that he had refused to go back to school. On the last day of school, when the auditorium was decorated with birch branches and the choir was getting ready to sing the spring hymn, Joona sneaked behind the curtains and slipped a homemade bomb under the piano. I didn't dare imagine what would have happened if the music teacher hadn't noticed it and if the chemistry teacher hadn't known how to defuse it. 'But he's very intelligent,' the women added. 'You can be proud of that.'

I was happy about the women's words. I was happy that everything wasn't my responsibility, that someone else was helping us get by. I was happy to believe that everything that happened was part of some passing phase, that time would pass and then ordinary life would start. In that life Joona would have children, go to work, exercise and pay taxes, and we'd gather to celebrate Christmases with three generations.

Even though that life never quite seemed to start, I didn't lose faith in it. Just this one more phase, this therapist, this conversation, and then. Just a little more time, and then we'd both enter into a calm and reassuring adulthood, where fear and anxiety would fall into perspective and everything could be worked out by talking about it.

On the eve of Christmas Eve, when I was a little younger than the girls in the yard of the children's hospital, I was still sure that that life would start some day.

Mother and Father were doing last-minute shopping and Joona and I were baking biscuits. Electric candles burned on the windowsill and the scent of the Christmas tree flooded in

59

from the living room. Joona lifted his eyes from the dough and asked whether I wanted to get high.

'What?'

'Get high. Smoke some dope. Hash. Drink a little Christmas hash tea.'

I was pressing fat-legged pigs into the rolled-out dough, and between them in the unused spaces, tiny moons. The dough smelled of cinnamon and cloves and the oven's warmth filled the kitchen. My Christmas would come tomorrow. We would sit together on the living-room sofa and watch the reading of the Christmas Peace announcement on television. Mother would be between Joona and me. She would put her arms around our shoulders. That would be my Christmas and even Joona would let us touch him. Father would serve pale mulled wine on a tray, and we would all keep our unspoken agreement. You don't fight at Christmas. No matter what happens, you don't fight at Christmas.

'Well?'

Joona crumpled up some dough as if planning to throw it. Behind his back hung a Boy Scout advent calendar, one square of which we got to open every day.

'Shouldn't we save that for New Year's? For that party you were talking about?'

'You're chicken.'

'I'm not chicken. I just don't feel like it right now.'

I pressed the cookie cutter into the dough with both hands. Joona tore off pieces of his dough ball and pushed them into his mouth. Tomorrow would be his turn to open a window of the advent calendar. A fat-cheeked baby would lie in a manger in a stable with his eyes closed and everything would be well.

'It's OK to admit you're chicken. I've always known you were. You're the one trying to say different.'

Tomorrow is Christmas. I tried to project that thought into Joona's head.

'You insist on being dragged along to everything fun. "Take me to the party!" I'd die of shame, the way you are.'

The smell of swede casserole. A one-legged elf on a branch of the Christmas tree. An angel bell. A box of chocolates. Ribbons for wrapping presents. The basket we carry the presents in. Please, Joona. Remember how nice things can be?

'Isn't it nice that we can bake biscuits and play house? A perfect Christmas. If you'd just…'

Don't. Ruin. This.

'I guess I'll have to tell Mika. That you're chicken to try anything.'

Mika. Mika was Joona's best friend. Mika's father was in jail and his mother had tried to commit suicide by putting her head in the gas oven. At night when I couldn't sleep I'd tell myself stories about Mika and myself. I'd bump into him in the street on a snowy evening. He'd be sad and try to hide it, but I'd see the frozen tears on his eyelashes. We'd walk together through the quiet streets and stop now and then to look at a single lighted window in an otherwise sleeping house.

After a while Mika would start to talk. He'd tell me about the nights when he lay awake holding his breath under the blanket and listen to his mother's footsteps. About brief visits to the prison's family room and the shirt his father wore when he was young. I'd listen quietly. When I'd slip, Mika would take my arm and steady me without noticing what he was doing. We'd walk through the streets all night, our hands warm, our fingers laced, and I'd find the right words to make him feel better. As the sun would rise Mika would understand that if he'd just let me, I'd know how to breathe new life into him.

Mika had just dumped his girlfriend. He was throwing a party on New Year's Eve and it was up to Joona to invite me.

'Why do you want to get high right now?'

'For Christmas. It'd be cool to do something with you. Without Mum and Dad knowing. Like when we were little.'

'Yeah.'

Joona boiled water for the tea. He went into his room and brought out something wrapped in aluminium foil. Inside the foil was a lump of something that looked like dried biscuit dough. Joona crumbled it into the hot water. Joona's mug had white hearts on a red background. Mine said *Mother*.

'To Christmas,' Joona said, and clinked his mug against mine.

'To the New Year's party,' I said.

'You've so got a crush on Mika.'

'I so do not. I hardly even know him.'

We drank the hash tea and reminisced about the summers when we'd ride up to the Arctic Ocean in a camper van and skip stones across the water with Father. Or Christmases when Mother and Father would sit hand in hand on the sofa and we'd secretly suck the fillings out of chocolates. Joona told me about a gang of boys that would sit on the granite out behind the house on Friday nights, drinking the raspberry wine that winos would buy them. Mika and Joona were the gang leaders. They knew how to walk along looking cool with a baseball bat or car aerial in their trouser leg and pull it out faster than anyone.

On weekends they had gang fights, punishing boys from some other school or part of town for something. Dozens of boys from middle school would meet at a certain place at a certain time with aerials, baseball bats, brass knuckles, chains, and switchblades. They talked about spin-kicks and broken teeth and noses as if it were all a comic book or a game where you got points for hits and the 'guys' were instantly good as new and there were never any real consequences.

While recovering from the last fight and getting ready for the next one, they drove around in stolen cars and threw parties where they got drunk and gave girls love bites. And I wanted to go too.

I wanted to sit on the granite next to Mika and let him put his arm around my waist. Leave the party with Mika and walk hand in hand through the falling snow and tell each other that we wanted more out of life than other people did. Sit in the back seat of a stolen car and drink beer out of Mika's bottle.

Joona didn't want me along. 'It's not for you,' he said. 'You're too sensitive. And I'd be embarrassed.'

But now we were drinking hash tea together and Joona promised to think again.

I can't remember anything. Can't tell if this is true or a dream. Deep down inside I feel like screaming. This terrible silence stops me. We were lying on the floor and Joona was holding my hand. His face was upside down and he looked old and frog-like.

We put Metallica's *One* on over and over and sang along. *Hold my breath as I wish for death. Oh please God, wake meeee!!!*

A straw mobile spun up by the ceiling. I spun on the floor. The walls were spinning. The bass boomed in my breast and belly. Joona squeezed my hand and we laughed till my stomach hurt.

'What the hell is going on here?'

Mud flew off the toes of Father's winter boots. Grey tracks were left on the just-washed rug. We lay on the floor and the tracks circled us. A burned smell floated in from the kitchen.

'The biscuits!' That was Mother's voice and it came from somewhere far off.

'What the *hell* have you two been doing?'

When Father lifted Joona off the floor and hit him in the face for the first time I was sure that he didn't see me at all. Joona's eyes were half closed. Blood trickled out of the corner of his mouth. 'Joona feels no pain,' I thought. 'Joona is so high that no pain can reach him.'

When Father hit him for the second time, Joona fell to his knees on the floor. His shirt rode halfway up his back and Father's shoe landed on his bare flesh. 'Henri!' Mother stood in the living-room doorway. The smell of the burned biscuits filled the room. 'Don't. You'll hurt his kidneys!'

Mother had a stained oven mitt on her hand and a black stripe on her cheek. Father's neck was dark red. Joona was bleeding onto the living-room rug.

I bent over to the floor and hugged Joona. He pushed me aside and got up. He was skinny and taller than Father. He knew how to crush a person's knees.

Joona stepped up to Father and kicked him in the shin. First lightly, as if to test whether it was possible. Father rocked back. He raised his hands halfway and looked for a moment as if he were about to say something.

The second kick looked like something from a karate movie and landed on Father's lip. There was blood on his chin. The third kick landed on his temple and dropped Father to the floor.

Father said nothing.

Mother said nothing.

Father shielded his head with his hands and Joona kicked him again. In the back, in the exact same spot where Father had kicked him.

Joona did not resist when I led him out of there. I held his hand and put on his bomber jacket and shoes. I took my own down jacket, a ski cap, and a scarf. Mother stood in the doorway. She was still wearing the oven mitt on her hand. The black stripe on her cheek had spread into a grey stain.

13

The display on my mobile phone is lit up. Mother is calling. I push the red button with my thumb, wipe my eyes on a napkin, and light a cigarette.

'He says you don't care about him any more.'

I didn't mean to turn back. I didn't mean to get up off the park bench, stuff my book in my bag, and sneak across the street to another café. No.

What I meant to do was gather my strength and walk to the hospital as if to an office, jacket open and scarf flung rakishly over my shoulder. 'Hello,' I meant to say. 'I'm Joona Louhiniitty's sister.'

I would have stayed forty minutes, maybe an hour, walked home, and then made pizza margherita with Ian. In the evening Ian would have stroked my hair, before falling asleep I might have said something about the hospital and cried a little. Just a little, like a little gulp of breath, not sobbing and moaning aloud and gasping for air. I would have cried as people do when they know they're almost over the grief and tomorrow will be an ordinary, tolerable day.

In front of me a cappuccino steams. The foam is as thick and firm as candyfloss. I burst the white peak with my spoon and drink the coffee aroma in through my nostrils. I press my palms against the cup's plump sides. They burn my skin.

What if Ian one day presses his palms against the sides of my belly just like this, trying to feel the tiny heart beating under the tight little mound? What if he one day presses his face against my skin, trying to smell through it the scent of new life? What if that day never comes? What kind of days will I have to live then?

14

'If we had a baby,' Ian said, 'what would we name it?'

He was lying on the sofa with his head on my stomach. I was twirling a sweaty lock of his hair around my finger. He wasn't wearing a shirt. He only had a few hairs on his thin chest. My fingertips knew those places by heart, just as I knew his earlobes, his collarbone, his buttocks, and the dry place in the curve of the small of his back.

We'd spent three days and nights in my apartment. Every now and then one of us had run to the shop, jacket open and shoes barely on, grabbed some French bread, grapes, blue cheese, and a box of expensive foreign strawberries, and dashed home with the bag of food. We had lain against each other, run our fingers along each other's skin, talked of childhoods and adolescences, of hurts and laughs and dreams. We had talked to each other as you'd talk to a stranger you'd met while drunk after the barman calls for last orders, sure you wouldn't remember the other's face in the morning.

Feeling Ian's skin under my fingers, I had begun to imagine a life for us. An old wooden house, a fire in the Dutch oven, Ian bent over a book and me with a mug of tea in my hand, looking out of the window. White stars and snow falling like stars, the warmth of the fire against my back and a moment, just that one moment, without fear of what might later happen.

Thoughts crawled into my mind all at once. Ian had imagined the same thing as I had. He too had had an image of a future with the two of us in it. The two of us fat, our skin slack, finishing each other's jokes. And: in his image there weren't just two of us, but more. Ian and I in a restaurant asking for a highchair, picking up toys left on the floor, waiting for a drunken teenager to come home.

I turned so his head slid off my stomach. I took my hand out of his hair and half sat up.

'We won't have kids,' I said. 'I couldn't. I'd be afraid to. Give life to something.'

Before Ian had a chance to say anything, I started telling him about my mother before she was my mother, back when she was a little girl with a desperate look and her hair pulled back too tight on her head.

Mother's father died in the war and her grandmother sent her to Sweden as a war orphan. Her new family lived in a wooden house painted red with Dutch ovens and white door trims like something out of Astrid Lindgren's *Noisy Village*. But the new family never really became her family. Evenings, when the others had gone to bed, my mother would sit alone by the window and dream of summers and Christmases to come, when her children would dance around the Christmas tree and they would all wear aprons made out of the same material.

Before she became our mother, for many years she loved an older man with black eyebrows and scars on his wrists who drank beer for breakfast and wrote poems about poverty and the revolution. Before she became a mother, she sat in a red Marimekko blouse with big white polka-dots on it on the man's bed and waited for him to stop writing and come to her.

When the man finally got up and sat down on the bed and unbuttoned her blouse, she hoped that what happened next would make her a mother. She hoped they would have a red-cheeked black-browed child who would make her feel whole and would make the man smile more easily than before. And the three of them would move out of the rented studio apartment in Stockholm into a wooden house that would smell of apples and spruce branches.

The man vowed that that would never happen. 'How the

hell could you want to bring kids into this world?' he asked, and turned his back on the woman. The woman clenched her fists.

When the man had said the same thing enough times, the woman stopped talking about it. But as she walked alone along snowy streets the woman stopped to look at the lighted windows with wooden lamps with red lampshades in them. She imagined the people living behind those windows, a mother and a father kissing their children good-night and sitting across from them in the glow of the lamp, reading books and sipping wine.

When the woman returned home from her walk, she found the drunken man sitting at the typewriter with a wine bottle and breathing heavily. Sometimes when the woman started a conversation about something, anything that would make the man smile or answer or draw an elephant or lion on her back, the man would smack his palm on the desk and shout.

'What the hell do you think you know about life?' he would ask, his eyes glittering like a stranger's. 'You want to drag everything around you into some cute little idyll where everything is clean and scented and everyone wants the best for everyone else. That's never going to happen. It's impossible. Get it? That idyll doesn't exist!'

When the woman had heard the same words enough times, when she had lain awake enough nights in the narrow bed looking at the man's back, she packed her big beaten-up suitcase and bought a ticket on the ferry to Helsinki.

The woman stood up on deck the whole trip, in the wind and the sleet. The ski cap her Swedish mother had knitted for her blew off into the sea. The woman gripped the railing with bare hands and the sleet falling on her face blended with her tears.

Many months after the ferry had arrived in the harbour, when the woman had unpacked her suitcase and tried to get to know her Finnish mother and to speak the Finnish language without a foreign accent, she went for a walk down to the seashore. It was a bright day in early autumn, she was wearing a light brown raincoat and a flowery scarf, and as she walked past the old stone buildings and old-fashioned street-lamps, she began to hear voices behind her.

The woman turned and saw a vociferous crowd of people approaching, carrying cardboard signs and chanting, 'Support the Czechs and Slovaks! Viva Dubček!' Hundreds of people marched in tight groups, some holding hands.

When the bulk of the marchers had passed, the woman pulled her scarf tighter around her neck. She felt a momentary surge of joy and experienced the sting of not belonging.

She was just wondering whether she'd have the courage to join the protestors, when she noticed a stern-eyed man at the end of the line. He walked a little apart from the others, his jacket open and his hands buried deep in his pockets. His voice was louder and deeper than the others, and his eyes were squinched into narrow streaks. Before the woman had had a chance to decide anything or think what she wanted to do, she found herself walking alongside the man and fitting her protests to the rhythm of his.

'I don't know whether I fell in love with your father,' Mother had told me years ago, when I forced her to tell me about the time before I existed. 'But somehow I started to feel like he might be the one to give me what I was hoping for.'

I hadn't even noticed that I had started to cry. Ian got up, grabbed some toilet paper from the bathroom, and brought it to me. I wiped my eyes and wondered how I would feel if he walked out and never came back.

'I've never dared ask how Mother thinks about all that now,' I said, crumpling the wet toilet paper in one hand. 'I mean, what the fulfilment of her dream was really like.' Ian took the wad of toilet paper from me and dropped it in the wastebasket, ran me a glass of water from the tap, and sat back down next to me. He moved around my apartment as if he belonged there, and it felt frighteningly good. 'What was it like?' he asked. He was quiet long enough that I dared tell the story.

15

It was the night before Christmas Eve. Joona walked ahead and spat on the ground while I concentrated on the fur-lined hood of his bomber jacket. I was still high. The streetlamps and the darkened windows in the houses surged around me, but I had to keep my mind under control. I had to concentrate on Joona's back and everything that had just happened at home. Somehow I had to make everything all right by morning.

On the church steps Joona turned around. The vapour of his breath softened the lines of his face.

'I want to be alone,' he said. 'Go home.'

I curled my toes inside my boots. The cold spread up from my legs into my hips and stomach. The toes of his army boots were crusty with dried blood. I looked at his swollen lower lip and the long hair hanging out of his hood. I hated him so much my lungs burned.

'Let's swap,' I wanted to say. 'You be me and I'll be you.

Let me go and kick in shop windows and spend the night in jail and wake up tomorrow morning with beer for breakfast. You be my sister and go home and clean up the mess.'

I nodded.

'Go then,' I said. 'Promise you won't do anything stupid.' Joona walked away without looking back, his hands deep in his pockets and his shoulders hunched so high it looked as if he had no head.

When he'd gone, I climbed up on the granite behind our house and lay down. Snow fell on my face. I closed my eyes and felt the snowflakes melting on my cheeks and forehead. I let my shoulders and hips drop heavily onto the cold ground, let my fingertips and toes lose all sensation and melt into the snow. I sank down through the icy crust deep into the bowels of the earth, into soft lava, which sucked me into its arms and rocked me gently so that the outlines of my skin vanished and only motion remained. I could see my body somewhere far away, a little hillock that the snow had wrapped in its pure veil.

In the early morning hours, when someone started banging on the door to the house, I wished I had dared to stay out in the garden – that I could rest under the snow till spring, knowing nothing of what was to come.

I heard Joona crashing around in the hall. I curled up

under my blanket and prayed that he would go into his own room quickly and I would soon hear him breathing evenly.

Joona's steps moved into the kitchen. He banged cupboard doors and drawers. I crossed my hands around my knees and said over and over: 'Dear God, show me that You exist. Let Joona go to sleep. Don't let Father wake up. If you exist, don't let anything bad happen now.'

I heard steps and scratching. Joona's breathing and a muttered curse. After a long silence, the pounding of my own heart. I smelled a tiny wisp of smoke as it made its way into my room. No. Not this. Please let me be imagining this. I smelled burning wood. I got up, opened my door and saw the flames. I saw Joona in front of the flames. He stood half-turned away from me and rubbed his eyes as if not quite believing what was happening in front of him.

The less oxygen a fire gets, the shorter time it will burn. The sentence was from Joona's elementary school science club assignment. I remembered the notebook's blue cover and Joona's round cursive, Joona in his flannel shirt with his glasses fixed with duct tape explaining how you could make a bubbling volcano with vinegar, baking soda, and dishwashing detergent.

'I'm going to be a scientist!' Joona had said.

'Remind me to buy a suit for the Nobel ceremony,' Father had smiled.

They had stood side by side at the kitchen table and Father had showed him how to start a steam engine with fuel pellets that looked like sugar cubes. I had hated Joona because Father tousled his hair and told him things about machines and science that he never told me. I had hated Father because he would go to the Nobel ceremony with Joona and I'd be stuck at home with Mother.

I pushed Joona away from where he stood in front of the Christmas tree, kicked over the burning tree, and smothered the flames with the living-room rug.

While I pushed the rug against the tree's smouldering trunk, I saw Father in the living-room doorway. He was missing a button on his pyjama top, and his temple, where Joona had kicked him, had a purplish bump and dried blood on it.

When Father stepped over the living-room threshold, I drew my hand across my throat like a knife and mouthed the silent words 'Stay out.' Mother pulled Father back into their bedroom. From behind the door I could hear fierce whispering. I tried to go to Joona.

'Don't,' Joona said. 'Don't touch me. Don't come any closer.' He sat on the floor with his face in his hands and trembled visibly. He had charred tinsel in his hair and all around him lay shattered glass angels and gold-trimmed baubles, half of them burned to a crisp. I sat next to him and blew my nose. A sooty streak was left on the tissue.

'Joona, please.'

'Don't even start,' Joona said. He pushed me away so hard that I toppled over. 'Don't give me your… I see right through you and… You have no idea what I… What's going on inside me.' I could see Mother's reflection in the hall mirror. She crept barefoot into the hall and lifted the telephone into the crook of her arm. Seeing me looking at her, she held a finger to her lips.

It's hard to remember what happened after that. When I try to remember, I'm not sure whether I am really remembering that night or some later one. Or something that I've just been afraid would happen, or invented afterwards.

This is what I remember:

From the bedroom come the sounds of a panicky argument and Mother's businesslike voice as she dials the emergency number and talks to the person who answers. Joona lets me hug him. His hair smells of outside air, soot, and Father's shampoo. By his thigh lies a one-eyed angel. I can see a convex reflection of the whole room in the remaining glass eye. The door bangs.

Another bang. Before my eyes appear four legs draped in

dark blue cloth. Joona tears himself out of my arms. I cover my ears with my hands and press my face into the sofa. I smell dust and the scent of some frail animal. Joona's shout cuts through my spinal cord.

Somewhere out past the rushing in my ears I can hear a siren. I raise my eyes and see the Christmas lights ringing the balcony railing. A blue flashing light slashes the white glow of the glass flames. When I stand up and press my face to the window, I see the red funnels of the tail lights on the ambulance and squad car vanishing into the Christmas dark.

I don't remember what Father and Mother and I talked about. Maybe we had a calm, rational conversation about the problem and treatment and how no-one had noticed in time. Maybe one of us said the words *mental hospital*. Maybe each of us wandered off to bed alone, unable to talk with or even look at anyone else.

When the night began to pale into morning, I crept into Joona's room, wrapped his bedspread around my shoulders, and curled up on the windowsill.

I didn't think of him. I didn't think of his yelling at the door, the hands gripped around his arms, the cars peeling out of the drive. I pressed my forehead to the glass and remembered a Christmas from many years before. Back when every Christmas was filled with magic. I linked my hands around my knees and saw a candle-lit church, old women dusting the snow off their mink hats, Father tall and white at the altar like an angel, and in the front pew, Mother, Joona, and me.

We're small and Mother has packed colouring books for us to take along. We're down on our knees colouring in between the lines with coloured pencils. Joona has his head leaning against my forehead, his hair tickles my temples. He's colouring an astronaut stepping onto moondirt, I'm colouring a shepherd girl in a frilly dress leaning on a shepherd's crook.

Father begins to talk. I lift my eyes from the shepherd girl and listen. Next to me sits an elderly woman whose skin is like tissue paper. She came into the church alone, stopped to breathe on every step, and gripped the railing with both hands. Her lips move to the rhythm of Father's words.

'The birth of Jesus is the celebration of grace,' he's saying. 'The celebration of the forgiveness of our sins.' I squint my eyes in the light spilling into the church through the high windows and see Jesus on the wall. He has red cheeks and a lined brow and he holds grace in his chubby hands.

Grace is round and copper-coloured. The same colour as Gran's hall lamp, which burns all night when I'm there and am afraid of nightmares. Grace's surface is spotted with star-shaped holes filled with pieces of green, yellow, and purple glass, through which star-shaped light floods out.

When we leave church, Father takes Joona and me by the hand. Snowflakes float in the calm air. When you stop and look up at the sky, you can almost fly towards them. 'Come on,' Father shouts, 'fairies from outer space are attacking! We have to save the earth!' We stick out our tongues to catch the fairies. Father holds our hands and we spin around with the snowflakes, cold drops on our tongues, and once, I'm sure of it, instead of a snowflake I swallow a star.

I pressed my face against my knees and remembered that Christmas so painfully that it had to be true. I hoped that Joona would remember the same.

16

I'd never been able to imagine it: a love that felt so absolute that I could be teary and chaotic and rest on the assurance that someone would hold me and want me to wake up in the morning next to him.

My relationships had been based on two things: tending to someone's needs, and despair. Cheeks burning, I went off with junkies who'd run out on rehab, car thieves awaiting prison sentences, and alcoholics dreaming of revolution. I was on constant full alert, ready to pay late bills or find the bag of amphetamines hidden in a bookcase. I loved that feeling of emergency, that moment when I could hold a man harassed by drug dealers, or the police, in my arms, stroke his panicky face, and tell him that we'd get through this. I loved nights that seemed to last twenty-four hours, when after fighting, fucking, and getting high I got to hear stories of loneliness, anxiety, and suicide attempts – and after all that, the words I had dreamed of hearing since my childhood: 'Without you I wouldn't even have the strength to try.'

The more bedraggled the man sleeping in my bed was, the more clarity I felt. I could feel that I represented a world filled with fresh air and long walks, healthy breakfasts and the hope that some day everything would work out. On the rare occasions when I tried to date men with well-behaved friends and plans for the future, I felt the dread of not belonging and being exposed as an impostor. I knew that it was only a matter of time before the man would see through me. He would see a family that could never pull off a light, friendly evening with his family, and a dark wind that could plunge me into chaos at any moment.

With Ian I was able for the first time to stop *managing* and live all the feelings that I had squirrelled away on the dark evenings when I had lain in bed with my fingernails in my palms and listened through the wall of the family room to Father's and Joona's increasingly heated voices. Because of that, I'd do anything for him.

It was night and Ian was at a literature department party. Often after these things he wouldn't be home till morning. He'd go out with colleagues and listen to someone playing old Finnish Stalinist records and someone else trying to translate the words into English.

This night he came home earlier than usual.

I was taking out the rubbish and ran into him at the front door. He stood there silently and held onto the doorjamb. His eyes were red and there was dried vomit on his jacket collar. When I went to him he held out his hand as if greeting a stranger. 'I'm sorry,' he said. 'So, so sorry.'

I led him inside and took off his jacket. He fell over on the hall rug. His lower lip was bleeding. I took off his shoes and scarf, picked him up by the armpits and dragged him to bed. He sat quietly on the edge of the bed while I washed the vomit off his neck and the corner of his mouth, pulled off his shirt and trousers, and tucked him in. He let me do everything as if I were a doctor or a nurse touching him professionally, as if we had signed a wordless agreement that this was actually not his body and that the hand that touched it did not in fact belong to anybody.

'What happened?' I asked. Ian asked for water. I got an old tin cup that I'd brought with me from home and held his head against my breast while I held the cup to his lips and let him drink like a small child.

When I thought he was already asleep and I had fallen asleep myself, sitting up with the empty cup in my hand, Ian opened his eyes. He began to talk about a cool night long ago, about the city lights and a boy who had suddenly felt alive.

*

'It was after Dad had come home. I tried to be invisible. Dad was seeing things and Mom was on edge. I tried to help with the chores and stay cheerful. So Mom wouldn't worry. The whole time it felt like I was choking.

'One night Dad was screaming. Mom crept in to give him some water. I lay there in bed with my eyes closed and listened to the voices from the next room. I tried to remember what it was like before Dad went to war. Were there moments when nobody was upset or worried about something? I couldn't remember. I still don't remember what our life was like back then.

'There was no oxygen left in the room. I opened the window and breathed the night air, but still I felt like I was suffocating. I decided to climb up onto the roof.

'It was a wispy foggy night, the sky full of city lights.

'When I lay back and closed my eyes, the lights turned into moving rings. All of a sudden the rings stopped. I kept my eyes closed. The stranglehold around my neck loosened. And...'

'And what?'

'Nothing. Damn. This sounds so stupid.'

'And what?'

'And the air flowed in.'

He was quiet for a moment, grabbed my hand, drew curved lines on my palm.

'For the first time I felt like I just *was*. Without being aware of myself every moment. I stopped thinking.'

His fingernails tickled the skin on my palm.

'I've never been able to go back to that state,' he said quietly. 'But that moment became my home. Every time I felt cut off, adrift, I would climb up on the roof and remind myself of that moment.'

'Even as an adult?'

'Until I left New York.'

He raised his head and looked at me as if he weren't sure who I was and why he was lying in my arms, cheeks wet and vomit on his breath. I wanted to give him a place where he could have that same feeling he'd had before.

Ian took a sip of water and shook his head when I tried to ask more. Then he began, quietly and stumblingly, to remember what it was like in New York after the terrorist strikes.

'Those days,' he said, 'those days and weeks, God, what grief. I was overflowing with it.'

He walked alone in the city, which was like somewhere out of a dream or a film, one of those countless films where America is threatened by some unknown danger and a shiny-haired man saves the day. He walked in the city and felt a ubiquitous feeling of togetherness, of belonging, which made people smile at each other more warmly, touch more easily and listen longer.

Ian met his friends whose family members or spouses had died in the twin towers. He drank wine and coffee with them, held their hands, let their tears wet his shirt, sat quietly for as long as they wanted to talk.

He met his mother, who had moved with Michael to a big house in the suburbs, where chestnut trees grew and the manicured lawn was surrounded by high walls. His mother was wearing a checked suit and earrings made of real pearls. She kissed Ian on both cheeks and reminded him to wash his hands before eating. Michael was wearing a grey suit and a pink dress shirt. He poured white wine for Ian's mother and whisky for himself and Ian, and unconsciously quoted the president's words.

He met his father. In the psychiatric ward of the veterans' home he found a man in a bathrobe whose voice was hoarse from smoking and who had forgotten to put on underpants under his robe. In the ward he found a bent-over man whom the nurse led back to get dressed, and who got slapped when he tried to pinch the nurse's thigh, who coughed and cursed and burst into tears, and who had not the faintest idea who had come to see him.

'You're very kind, young man,' he said when Ian combed his hair into the same kind of wave he remembered from pictures of his youth, and trimmed his long fingernails. 'I wish you could stay longer.' They walked down the hall to the TV room, his father's hand firmly in the crook of Ian's arm.

'We've got to save the world,' his father said. They sat in the TV room with the other men in their bathrobes and slippers and watched the president stand among the ruins of the towers in a fireman's helmet and a windbreaker and speak encouraging words. 'It's a shitty job. I'd rather hawk loogies at the ceiling and let the globs drop on my face. But what're you gonna do? Somebody's gotta fight on the front lines.'

'Really?' Ian asked, squeezing his dad's lumpy hand. 'Is that what you thought when you were leaving for Vietnam?'

His father didn't answer for a long time. Then he pulled his hand away and looked at Ian through blurry eyes. 'Boom boom. Bam bam. God damn. Another rain of lead and another soldier's dead,' he half-sang, pointing his finger at Ian like a gun. 'I'm hit, I'm hit, I'm in a world of shit, somebody blew up the whole fucking shitter.'

Ian led his father back to his own room, read him the joke column and the horoscope out of the paper and tucked him into bed. 'It was very nice talking to you, young man,' his father said as Ian buttoned his coat at the door. 'Very, very nice.' Ian nodded his agreement, waved his hand, and disappeared at a half-run into the cold, neon night of New York.

'This is so stupid,' Ian said. His mouth was on my thigh and his warm breath tickled my skin. 'It feels like that was the first time I realized that Dad would never get better. That until that moment I'd somehow imagined that…'

'That you'd be able to save him?'

'Yeah. And then. Then I realized that I wouldn't. That he would never remember me. And tonight.'

'Tonight?'

'Tonight I realized that there's nothing. No place.'

He turned his back on me and curled up into the fetal position, arms wrapped around his shins. My Ian. Wise, calm Ian, who had led me into a world where you could have panic attacks and nightmares and still know that somewhere there was a hand that would wipe your tears, that would wake you at night and walk you to the window, and show you how the moon illuminates the building across the way and a little stretch of street.

My Ian shook and sobbed like a baby, and there was nothing I could do but hold him until my arm went numb and my neck hurt when I turned my head.

17

Mr Caretaker,

I'm writing to straighten out a misunderstanding according to which I tried to burn down the bike cellar in our building. There are all kinds of rumours flying around about me and it doesn't always feel very good. But that evening I wasn't even in the building and my mother can vouch for that.

On the other hand I wish you would pay more attention to how the kids in the yard (who I believe were responsible for this rumour) behave: they never greet me (though I always greet them nicely as I do everybody else who lives in the building, because I think it makes people feel good)!

Instead, when I walk by they stare at me and then start giggling. That feels bad, especially since I have NOT done anything bad to them. Week before last they came and giggled outside my door, and last night one of them sneaked in through my window and stared at me next to my bed all night.

Do you think that's right?

Respectfully yours,
requesting swift action,
Joona Louhiniitty

18

'Would you like anything else, ma'am?'

The waiter raps on the table and I realize that he must have been standing there for a while, with a full ashtray in his hand, glancing out of the corner of his eye over at the man at the next table calling for his bill. I would. I would like to know at what point I lost Joona. When did I stop going home and returning his phone calls? When did I stop hoping that something would change? When did I decide to live as if he had never existed?

'Yes?'

'Sorry. Campari on the rocks.'

On that September day when the planes crashed into New York's towers and more than three thousand people died, Joona called and I answered.

He had visited me the previous evening. I had made stuffed crêpes and helped him write a personal ad for the internet. *Sensitive, shy, lonely man seeks understanding woman. I don't enjoy going out to bars, but I'll understand if you want to party. I dream of having a family and an ordinary life.* Joona had expensive clothes and new medication, which didn't make his face swell up and didn't slur his speech. Clicking Send on his ad, I could almost imagine the woman who would fall for Joona as for any other man and with whom Joona would at last dare to leave home. I could imagine Joona's family and ordinary life.

In the morning, waiting for a tram, I told myself stories about a Joona who got out of bed, went to the shop, and took the tram without sweating and making other passengers decide to sit somewhere else. This other Joona had a nice haircut and clean teeth and a wife who talked with him about politics, poems, and the structure of the universe.

On that September day, when Joona spoke into the phone with his panicky voice, when I left my lecture with my backpack open and flagged down a cab, on that day I still believed that that other Joona was waiting for us somewhere.

On Mannerheimintie the cab stopped at a light. The display window next to us had wide-screen televisions.

'Look,' the driver said.

On the screens a jet crashed into a tall office building. The sky was yellow and grey from the explosion.

'An ad for some new American film,' I said. 'Hey, it's green.'

The driver turned on the radio. A man's voice was talking about planes and towers, no word yet on how many dead. In the mirror I saw the driver's eyebrows go up. Outside the cab windows, yellow trees, the stadium tower, and the lights on the ferris wheel flashed by. The driver kept repeating, 'Damn, Jesus Christ, it can't be true.' I bit my tongue. 'Shut up,' I wanted to say. 'Turn off the fucking radio and drive: take me to Joona.'

Joona was sitting on the floor. His hair was dirty and he was in a striped bathrobe. Next to him were a fallen coffee cup and shards of a broken mirror.

The mirror had been clear and unframed, almost the size of the entire wall. It had made the apartment look bigger, the narrow hall like a large foyer. As a child Joona had made speeches in front of it and I had stuck my arms through under his arms from behind his back. We had been Charlie Chaplin, pop singers, President Kekkonen. Joona had borrowed Father's glasses, pulled a broken basketball over his head like a bald scalp, and said: 'Citizens, *medborgare*.'

Now the mirror was smashed on the floor and Joona's hand was bleeding. 'They fell,' Joona said. 'They fell and died, and no-one could help them.' I went into the kitchen and got a broom and a dustpan, swept up the shards and cleaned his wounds.

When we were in the cab to the hospital, Joona started talking about this man. His hand was in my lap and bled on my thigh through the paper, the bandage, and my jeans. The man's voice on the radio spoke of planes, the WTC, the president, rescue operations, and thousands of casualties, and gradually it began to sink in that a terrible thing had happened outside our home as well.

When Joona began to talk about the man, the driver turned the radio down. I squeezed Joona's hand, trying to get him to talk more quietly or wait till we were alone. He didn't wait. In a loud, colourless voice he told me about the man who had looked at him from the hall mirror. The man had a thin face and a sad look, his eyes had stared right through Joona. The eyes would not leave him alone, though he turned away and broke the mirror. They still wouldn't leave him alone, here in the cab: they were staring at him from the rear-view mirror and the dim reflection in the window.

'It'll pass,' I said, and stroked his hand. 'The medication will make it go away and then everything will be fine again.'

Joona shook his head. 'It won't. I don't want it to.'

'What?'

Joona didn't seem to notice the edge to my voice. He kept talking in a monotone, to everyone and no-one.

'I don't want this to pass. I've just now started to figure out who I am.'

I looked at Joona. His beard was unshaven and his teeth were covered with yellow sludge. His face was covered with tiny cuts from the mirror. Through the bathrobe I could smell his unwashed skin. Suddenly it seemed to me I was seeing him for the first time.

A sentence came to me as if I had heard it on the radio: *Her brother is mentally ill.* I pressed my forehead to the cab window. *She's taking her brother to the mental hospital.* She. I.

I tried to remember when I had really seen Joona last. I remembered only his childhood face, his serious look and the red splotches that decorated his cheeks when he got excited. That September day, in that taxicab hurtling across Helsinki towards the hospital on the other side of the park, I stopped seeing Joona as a little boy whom adulthood and the future awaited somewhere. That day I saw him for the first time as a man with a dirty beard and skin that smelled of illness. At the same moment I saw myself as a woman whose whole life was in danger of drowning in that man's sick-smelling world.

The cab stops at a light by the park. The woman tears at a chapped place on her lip. She looks out: the trees and the benches are still there; people are walking about in the park and children are riding around and around on the carousel that you push with little pedals. The woman says nothing, but you can see from her look that something inside her, something that she has been trying to protect against all evil, is dying.

We rode the rest of the way without talking. Joona's warm blood turned my stomach. I opened my window for some fresh air. At a bus stop I heard a woman speaking English into her mobile phone and crying.

19

Hey 'Waterbird'!

I turned this machine on again sweaty with anticipation. Maybe there's another message from you? I guess I have to stop hoping you'll ever write to me again.

It was probably a mistake to tell you about my illness.

You seemed so different from the others: deeper and more sensitive. When you wrote that externals aren't important, that what's important is what's inside, I got a warm feeling: I thought that you'd understand what's inside me.

Apparently I was wrong and now I understand: you're just like all the other women. I'll never trust anyone again.

Broken inside,

J

20

The display on my mobile phone is flashing SWEETIE. Ian's calling. SILENCE. I don't feel like talking now.

It's dark outside and people are on their way home from work. My novel lies face down on the table. Next to it is a full ashtray and a brown ring from my coffee cup. I count the cigarette butts: twelve. I've smoked twelve cigarettes but have not read a single full page of my novel. I have not fished the Dictaphone out of my bag and transcribed a single line of the MP's interview, though the story has to be finished in two days. I haven't gone to the hospital. Aside from my mother and the waiter, I haven't talked to anybody.

I've spent the day sitting in cafés and watching through dirty windows as people run for buses and trams in order to get to work on time. I watch them now as they run to get home or somewhere else where someone is waiting for them, waiting to transport them out of the working world and into some other world and time that will etch a deeper trace into their minds than work ever can. I've watched people running exhaustedly, enthusiastically, or desperately, and people moving without hurrying, keeping their eyes on the ground or far away in the air and walking along the very edge of the pavement as if wanting to melt into the stone walls.

On the other side of the glass time has moved forward, through consultations and lunches and recesses and meetings. My time has not moved all day. My time is a coffee stain dried on the table, mascara on my cheek, a battery bar that has disappeared from the display on my mobile phone. A breath during which the clear morning has turned into the heaviness of afternoon. A moment during which a cup of coffee has cooled and memories from years ago have clawed their way into consciousness. A city where a flood has overnight wet the floors of the houses and people walk through the streets calf-deep in water with bundles on top of their heads; clean trousers and an expensive drill bit, a certificate from an English language course, a present from a rich relative who lives far away. They hold their bundles with calm looks on their faces and walk on without knowing where and how their lives will be able to go on.

I've lost control of time and have not accomplished a single thing all day.

Maybe I'll never accomplish anything ever again.

I can see how my editor raps on the desk as he waits for the story that I'm never going to give him. How his ears turn red as he tries to call me, but my phone doesn't answer, and finally how he hires someone else, someone better and more reliable, to write that story on a tight deadline.

I see him erasing my name from the freelance list and sending out an email to his colleagues: *Anna Louhiniitty is an unpredictable and unreliable reporter. Don't give her assignments.*

I see Ian coming from the university to an empty apartment. How he sits for a moment by the window, and finally packs his bags.

How my friends after a few months or even a few weeks shrug their shoulders and delete my name and number from their phones.

How my account information is cleaned off the bank's computers and my name and social security number are sold to an illegal immigrant.

How Joona one day, years from now, sits up in his hospital bed and says: 'My sister. Why doesn't my sister care about me any more?' A passing nurse wrinkles her brow, turns around and rushes into the doctor's office. The doctor raises her eyes and asks: 'Again?' The nurse nods. 'Again.'

Two male nurses hold Joona tightly as another nurse pulls his hospital trousers down off his waist and jabs the strongest possible anti-psychotic drug into his buttock. After the injection Joona shouts, but the nurse takes his head in her lap and strokes it as I always have. 'Anna!' Joona shouts, and the nurse presses his head onto the pillow, closes his eyelids, and tells him to sleep. 'You're in a psychosis now,' the nurse whispers and runs her fingertips over Joona's scalp. 'You'll sleep peacefully. When you wake, you'll remember that you have never had a sister.'

21

'Shall we go?' Ian says.

'You decide.'

'You want to go.'

'Don't you?'

It was a Sunday in late winter and we'd slept in. The sun spread in squares across the kitchen floor and sleepy jazz played on the radio. We were sitting at the table reading the paper. It told about a war that was ready to start and today's demonstrations. People around the world were taking to the streets to protest against the war. They would have megaphones and banners and would shout slogans.

It would probably be bigger and better than demonstrations had been in a long time. Bigger than the peace marches that had been attended for years by no more than a handful of old hippies and young activists. Definitely bigger than the demonstrations against animal testing or globalization that sent out into the Helsinki streets the same small crowds of people in army jackets, ski caps, and heavy shoes. It would hardly be as wild and fiery as the demonstrations in cities where the world's most important leaders gathered to make decisions and where the police wore riot helmets and some demonstrators carried stones. But it could be as big as the demonstrations long ago, when Ian's mother carried him in a baby backpack.

'I'm not sure,' Ian said. 'I'm a little nervous about it.'

I closed the paper. Ian had croissant crumbs at the corner of his mouth and dried jam on his cheek. He looked down and tore at the cuticles on his right hand with the nails of his left. A tiny spot of blood welled up at the edge of one nail. I pulled my chair over to him and took both his hands.

'What?'

'Don't be angry.'

'Angry?'

He wiped the jam off his cheek, looked past me at the doorway or the wall and began to tell me about the literature department party from which he had come home with a bloody lip and vomit on his collar.

The boy was Ian's favourite student. He thought he saw in the boy's arrogance something of the same outsider feeling that he himself had always felt. He thought he saw in the boy something that required special encouragement and care, something he needed to work to bring out.

At the party the boy sat at Ian's table ordering beer and hard liquor. He was drunk and quieter than usual. Ian rambled on about fairly ordinary things, classes, the winner of the newspaper's short story contest. The boy said nothing. Ian drank more and talked more and faster, unable to stop, though he didn't really feel like talking at all.

Finally the boy stood up.

'Aren't you ashamed?' the boy asked.

'Excuse me?'

'Aren't you ashamed? You sit here with your mouth running, even though your country is about to bomb the world to shit.'

The boy spoke loudly and people at the next table turned to look at Ian. Ian opened his mouth. He had been expecting something like this.

When he had the flu, sitting there with a coffee cup in his hand and a blanket around his shoulders watching the television clips over and over of the twin towers collapsing into rubble, a single thought crept into his mind first, before the shock, the horror, the worry, and the grief. The thought sprang forth instantly when he turned on the television and understood what had happened. It took the form in his mind of a news story title, even before he had begun to process what he was seeing. *Everyone will hate us. America at War. Everyone will hate us.*

Everyone will hate us. The sentence ran through his mind as he ran through the streets with his jacket buttons half undone, out of breath and unsure where he was heading. He kept seeing it when he stopped on a bridge to look at the dark water and the lights burning on its surface like stars. He kept seeing it when he stopped at a kiosk to buy a cup of coffee and saw an old black woman burst into tears as she paid for her paper, and the vendor taking a bottle of brandy out from behind the counter, squeezing the woman's shoulder, and pouring her a shot.

Hate us. Ian studied the thought as he read endless speculations in the papers on how the strikes had been made. He soon knew who had done it, how they'd got into the country, where they had studied. He felt a grudging respect mixed with confusion and horror that they had been able to live so long in America without revealing their intentions to anyone. How they had talked to their fellow students, teachers, and neighbours, how they had partied and made love with Americans, all the while knowing that every moment they spent in America was part of their countdown to a single moment that would shake the entire world.

Soon Ian knew enough about the strikes that they became

a movie in his head (initials exploding into drops of blood? No, too corny. Introduce the principals in a rapid montage, each clip freezing at a crucial moment? Rammstein's music? No, been done) and kept running there without his being able to control it or decide when he wanted to watch it. He loathed it. It disgusted him that everybody was talking about *how* but all too few, at least publicly, asked *why*?

When his country began to move troops into Afghanistan, Ian thought he would suffocate under the weight of his questions.

He didn't think America shouldn't go to war. He thought they should have done that long ago. It revolted him that the world had put up with mass murders and rapes, floggings for listening to music or talking too loudly, punitive surgery, and the degradation of women. That none of *that* had made anyone want to go to war against the Taliban. He was disgusted by the hypocrisy of the American rationale for going to war, and by the consequences that it would have, but he could understand all that.

What he didn't understand was Iraq. He could not stand the thought of it. The feeling that somehow he would be personally responsible for what would happen in Iraq. How the war would destroy lives and minds, how its shadows would fall over the years and decades to come. How they would destroy, in ways that could not be foretold, the lives of generations to come.

Ian didn't speak of this with anyone. Over and over he had conversations with Finns that began with the words 'I just don't understand you Americans…', and noticed that he found himself defending something that he didn't understand himself. He couldn't stand it that everybody came to him to ask why Americans were such idiots-imperialists-warmongers, but nobody asked what he thought and how it all felt to him.

Ian looked at the boy's pale face, his thin beard and red dyed hair. The boy downed the liquor in his glass with one gulp. Ian was drinking wine.

The conversation around them had died down. People sipped their drinks, the ends of cigarettes glowed in the dark. The mood was thick with expectation, which they tried to hide behind surreptitious glances, small talk, and fiddling with fingers, anything that would hide the fact that they were all waiting to hear what Ian would say. And that the question and the silence it provoked had slammed them onto different sides, Ian alone on one, where he had to answer for the policies of his whole country, and maybe something else as well, something larger, and the others on the other side, where they could slosh wine around under their tongues and wait.

Ian would have loved to discuss it. He would have loved to have a discussion about the weight that had settled on him after the strikes, that had made it harder for him to breathe and walk. He would have loved to discuss history, American identity, and the questions no-one was asking. And tall towers whose roofs sketched a broken outline across the sky. A café that on Sundays served thick pancakes and fresh blueberries. The long skewers in a Chinese street kitchen, and a toothless woman who sold poems in the park. The scent of clean clothes flooding out of laundries. The bushy beards of black-clad Jewish men and a half-deaf Romanian who drove a long car with the stuffing coming out of its seats and called it a limousine. And the stare the black woman who cleaned the public spaces in his apartment building directed at him and to which he never knew how to respond.

Ian wanted to discuss all of that. And how, walking home in the evenings in the Helsinki streets and smelling the fries and the sea and the urine in the gateways, he could almost smell behind them the scents of another, larger city.

Ian wanted to talk about all this so desperately that he felt like shouting it, bellowing it out so loudly that the weight would lift off him and his voice could at last flow freely. But the boy's big grey eyes locked onto his and he asked again, even more aggressively than before:

'Aren't you ashamed that your country is the biggest asshole slimeball rogue state in the world?'

The uneasy silence at the tables around them turned into open expectation, but Ian still could say nothing. He stood up to refill his glass. When the others were looking the other way, he grabbed the whole cardboard wine box and slipped out with it under his arm.

The night sky was clear and sparkled with stars. His breath came out in great white clouds. Ian folded his scarf into a cushion and sat on the steps. He lifted the wine box to above his mouth, opened the spigot, and let the wine flow in. He drank down big gulps, swallowed, and burped. When he lowered the box to the step for a moment he could see on the insides of his eyelids the boy's pale face and self-sufficient smile. Behind them appeared yet other faces as well.

'Aren't you ashamed?' the faces mouthed. 'Aren't you ashamed that you have thick glasses and a crappy haircut and you've never been kissed by a girl? Aren't you ashamed that your dad's a nutjob and your mom's a druggie whore?' Ian pressed his fists against his eyes and tried to drive the faces out of there, back to the school corridors and dark corners of his building's courtyard, or into the pickle factories, hamburger joints, and restaurant doorways where they later ended up. He pressed his fists against his eyes and tried to push the faces back to a time he didn't want to remember. But they would not go away, and the words they chanted at him came now in his own voice: 'Aren't you ashamed that you left your father alone in an institution, and have absolutely no idea how he's doing? Aren't you ashamed that you failed at the one thing you should have taken care of?'

When Ian opened his eyes, the pale face was in front of him.

'Oh, you're out here,' the boy said. Ian set the wine down. The boy had one mitten balled up in his hand. 'Sorry if I offended you.'

Ian stood up. The faces were still there. All the faces. All the mouths. All the croaking voices, and his own loudest of all. The little boy with his hands clenched in fists, accusing his adult self of wasting his life. He felt dizzy. 'Do you hear me? Hey, what's wrong with you? Hey.'

He pushed the boy away. The boy stumbled. 'Hey, don't.'

Pissy voice. Pissy smile. All those pissy voices. Ian grabbed the boy by the shirt front, got right in the boy's face. The words came out as if he had rehearsed them.

'You're damn right I'm ashamed,' he said. 'If only you knew how much. I'm so ashamed that I want to throw a rope

113

around my neck and string myself up over that door there and you'd see it, and you… you have no fucking clue what you're talking about.'

He had never hit anyone before. His bony white palm jumped up, took momentum from the air, and smacked the boy in the face.

The boy's head snapped back. There was an icy silence. Then the boy burst into disbelieving laughter, pulled himself away from Ian, and ran out onto the slippery street with his jacket open.

'Why didn't you tell me before?' I asked.

Ian's hand trembled.

'Why didn't you tell me right then, when you got home?'

'I wanted to,' Ian said, fiddling with his newspaper, 'but I couldn't. And somehow. I can't explain.' A blush spread up to his ears. 'I felt the same as when I was a kid. When I'd wet the bed or stolen some gum.'

I got up, pulled Ian's head into my lap, and started stroking his hair, his temples, the back of his neck, his back. I felt the warmth of his breath against my stomach. I wanted to scrunch him up inside my hand and hide him somewhere, anywhere, so I could protect him against all evil. I stroked the hair off his face and kissed his forehead, cheeks, and mouth.

'Darling,' I said, and made him look at me. 'I love the child that you were. Everything about him. And everything that you are now.'

Ian caressed the bones in my face with his forefinger slowly, as if sketching me into existence.

'Let's go,' he said. 'To demonstrate.'

22

You fucking whore, don't you see how fucking easy your life is?

I have NEVER been able to travel alone. I have NEVER gone to a music festival or had a girlfriend. (Junior high doesn't count.)

You've become the same kind of asshole overachiever as everyone else, and if you don't reply to this I NEVER want to have anything to do with you. Then I won't have any sister at all and it'll be all the same to me if you're killed or raped or sliced up alive, I couldn't care less.

Fuck you,
Joona

23

We walked behind the demonstrators.

People were carrying black flags painted with white peace signs and yellow and red banners saying NO ATTACK ON IRAQ. The men walking in the front of the procession were kicking empty oil barrels and the car leading the procession had exploding red lights on its roof.

Ian had pinned a flea market peace sign to his lapel and I had wrapped an ancient Palestinian shawl around my neck. In front of us walked a group of boys dressed in army jackets and ski caps and carrying a large black flag saying HUMILI-ATING GENERATIONS: THE AMERICAN WAY. Ian read the words with a solemn look and I started talking incessantly to take the shadow out of his eyes:

'Wow, look at all these people,' I said. 'I can't remember the last time there were this many.'

And: 'Look at that baby. Is that what you looked like in the Vietnam demonstration?'

And: 'Hey, did you see the boy with the black ski cap and army jacket? Haven't we seen him somewhere before?' And: 'Man it's cold. After this is over you wanna go somewhere for a cup of hot chocolate?'

And: 'Listen, we don't have to be here if you don't want.'

We walked down streets emptied of cars from Rautatientori Square to the American embassy and shouted in unison: NO ATTACK ON IRAQ! In front of the embassy it was snowy and slippery and a fence kept the demonstrators out. We stood in wet snow up to our mid-calves and shouted as loudly as we could. A boy in dreads played the bongos, middle-aged women danced with their arms around each other's waists, and for a moment the whole demonstration felt at once like an important event and a kick-ass carnival that might just accomplish something.

I didn't notice him until he was so close that we couldn't turn away.

He was alone. He stood beside us and blew warm air on his fingers. His nails were brown and there was a tobacco stain on his right forefinger. He had clouded eyes and wore a terrycloth bathrobe. Crowded as it was around the front of the embassy, around him there was a vacant space.

24

ONE MESSAGE RECEIVED:

SWEETIE

Honey, please call or text me and tell me all is OK! Worried! Love.

I reply:

All is OK. Just busy with the article. Hugs.

The tears come as the envelope flies away on my phone display. I squeeze the wineglass between my hands and wonder how it would look if I squeezed harder. So hard that the glass shattered and sliced open my palm and the wine and blood spattered in clear drops on my blouse and the table.

25

He was supposed to be in the hospital.

He was supposed to be sleeping in a white room behind locked doors and balconies wrapped in barbed wire. To take his medications from blue plastic bottles morning, noon and night, meet the doctor once a week, and paint his feelings in art class. Walk down the corridor in his towelling dressing gown and slippers printed with the hospital's name. He was supposed to walk from his room to the smoking balcony and back with slow steps and stop to play ping-pong or chess with a man who years ago saw a documentary about a baby elephant that got lost from its mother, and who had had no other home than the hospital ever since.

'Anna, what is it?' Ian asked. I saw his tall figure next to Joona's delicate one, the tails of Joona's bathrobe behind Ian's army jacket.

I heard his voice and the sounds of the bongos, the wind, the chanting. I saw an old woman with a dog watching the demonstrators, straightening her scarf, a small boy in a baby sling on his mother's chest, a man's arm around a woman's waist, the stripes left by the muddy snow on suede bootlegs, all these people around me full of memories, disappointments, dreams, the air thick with them.

I saw Ian's questioning eyes.

'What is it?' I nodded at the man standing a few metres away from us, wearing a flapping bathrobe and hospital slippers, whose chest and legs were red with the cold and who knew more about me than anyone else.

I wanted to spirit him away to safety.

I wanted to wrap Joona up in my scarf and carry him to a safe place like the sparrow with a broken wing that we'd found on the granite in our back garden when we were kids, whose grave we had lined with cotton, leaves, and golden tinsel from the Christmas tree. I let go of Ian's hand, stepped past the boy throwing snow, the rasta girls and the old woman, and hugged Joona. His skin was cold. His eyes were wild and his voice desperate.

'Hide me,' he said. 'You have to.'

His heart pounded against my cheek and I remembered the time when my heart had been pounding just like this and Joona had come to save me.

*

I was in junior high and had arranged a birthday party.

At first I was afraid to. The boys in my class wore wide-leg track suits and hooded bomber jackets, the girls tight jeans and blue mascara. I wanted to look like them. I wanted to learn how to stand like them, back bent, hipshot. I wanted to learn to sound as natural as they did: 'So this morning Ma's all like you're not fucking putting juice on your Weetabix!' and 'So he's all I'll tell you in three days if we're going steady and now it's been two and a half and I'm like ready to slit my throat.' I wanted them to talk about me the same way they did about others: 'Who's coming?' 'Anna and them.' Or: 'Spent the weekend with Anna and them.' I wanted just one of them to talk to me.

I bought new jeans, the same straight-leg kind the other girls were wearing. I bought blue mascara and pink lip gloss and taught myself to pinch cigarettes from the shop next to the school.

'Having a party Saturday,' I said. I tried to sound cool. I stood there where the girls went to smoke and offered them stolen cigarettes. As they took them, they had stopped looking past me and started randomly saying hi and asking me what time it was.

'Gonna be booze?'

'Brother's getting some.'

122

The girls raised their eyebrows and looked at me as if trying to figure out whether I was telling the truth, or, I hoped, whether they had misjudged me, whether beneath my nervous shell I was after all a mysterious hipster.

I cleaned my room. I replaced the Sex Pistols posters on the wall with Madonna, carried my Edith Södergran poetry books to the attic and filled the record shelf with AC/DC, borrowed from Joona. When I pulled on my tight Levis that evening, and teased my hair up into a big bouffant, and dabbed on the lip gloss, I thought I looked almost believable. Like a girl who could bum money in the station tunnel or come to school two hours late with a bandana covering up her love bites.

The party was set to start at seven. I'd had two glasses of punch and dabbed on more lip gloss three times. I had crisps and the punch bowl on the table, and I saw myself as the main character in a film, a shy girl whose true life would begin any moment now. I saw the expressions of the class toughs as I opened the door in my new do, smiling a self-assured smile. A fast montage of hands dipping punch, crushed crisps on the floor, swaying hips, and surreptitious, embarrassed, and admiring looks directed at me. My own face at a solitary moment off in one corner, looking out over the room triumphantly, and then, a moment later, slipping into a bedroom hand in hand with the boy all the other girls have crushes on.

At seven-thirty my stomach started to hurt. I walked from kitchen to hall to living room, looking out of the windows. I counted cars.

'After five red ones have passed, they'll come.'

'After the next bus.'

'After two semis and one delivery van.'

'After the next police car.'

At nine I was sitting on the windowsill with my face against my knees, crying so hard I couldn't breathe.

When I could no longer be bothered to check the time, when my mascara was running in rivers, when the punch bowl was empty and I had vomit on the hem of my blouse, the doorbell rang.

They were drunk. They came in wearing their coats and boots and left muddy tracks on the floor.

'Check it out, Anna made-up.'

'Check out her face!'

'She's been howling here alone all evening!'

'Where are your friends?'

I had no time to hide anything. They saw everything, pathetic as it was. They saw my fallen hairdo, the mascara all down my cheeks, the smeared lipstick, and the too-new jeans.

They saw right through me, and I had nowhere to hide.

'Don't.'

'This is what you wanted.' The boy pushed me up against the wall with his hand. His other hand slipped under my blouse. The others watched from the floor, with the bowl of crisps and the shards of the broken punch bowl between them.

'You wanted romance, didn't you? All this work, so someone would notice you?'

'Please.'

'I'm making you feel good.' The boy's hand was cold, his breath in my face sharp. This is not happening to me, I thought. I'm not here. The hand is not touching me. This is not me shouting.

'What the hell's going on here?'

The boy's hand stopped. I opened my eyes and saw Joona. He stood behind the boy in his bomber jacket and boots and looked angry and big enough to lift the boy in the air with one hand.

Next to Joona stood Mika, in a hood, his dark hair half-covering his eyes. He looked at me through his hair. No-one said a word. I heard fast breathing and a thud as someone set a beer bottle on the floor. Joona and Mika were the best fighters in our part of town. They had a *rep*. When they stood in the living room with their lips tight and their eyes angry, and when Joona lifted his hand and grabbed the boy by the scruff of the neck, I had more power than I'd ever had before.

Joona bent the boy's arm behind his back and made him turn and look at him, Joona.

'Kneel,' he said. 'Kneel down and tell Anna you're sorry.'

'You're kidding.'

'It'll make you feel good.'

Joona's arm pushed the boy to his knees, so low that his lips kissed the floor. Mika came and stood next me, blew the hair from his eyes, put his arm around me. I became the main character in a film again. I was the girl who'd make it after all.

Now Joona's heart pounded against my neck and it was in my power to take him away.

26

President George Bush,

I'm writing to you to warn you of the consequences your planned attack on Iraq will have. You didn't take seriously the letter I wrote to you during the Afghanistan war, so: you're a murderer. The Disease of the Modern World.

This is not a game. PEOPLE die there. Am I a worse person to tell you this just because for a long time I haven't seen anything but these walls outside my head and everything inside them? Or is my voice the sound of silence that you must listen to?

I CAN FEEL IT when they're shot.

Life is not a Grand Narrative, Mr Bush. Inside these walls that's very clear. I must fight against your Narrative.

I've thought of self-deception as an existential question. Your self-deception is beyond the pale. It's a denial of the value of other people's existence and by killing others you deny your own value.

Generations and generations will follow whose memories you destroyed before they were even born. You Will Not Be Forgiven.

God must punish you. Someone has to.

Sincerely yours,
Joona Louhiniitty
Finland, Europe

27

Outside the café, knocking on the window, there's a woman with snarly hair holding a sign with the fat letters *I am the Way, the Truth, and the Life.* She looks at me with pale eyes and smiles as if she knows something. I look away, over to the café magazine rack, the news magazines staring back at me with men in black suits on their covers. Behind them I see my Joona in his hospital bathrobe, on the evening before the demonstration.

He's on his way to the balcony. His eyes are sleepy and he has a cigarette hanging between two fingers. He passes the nurses' booth, through the glass wall sees a television showing a light-haired woman with a tear running down one cheek. He stops. His gaze tracks over from the woman's delicately beautiful face to the nurses' hair, the bun combs and the dandruff glittering on their white coats in the harsh light, the dirty coffee cups, the medicine vials, over to the paper lying open on the counter.

Stop the war — No attack on Iraq. Demonstration meets 15 Feb at 2 p.m. at the Rautatientori Square. A cold tremor shoots through his belly. He's been waiting for this. He has lain awake at night, looked out of the window at a strip of starry sky, the lamp cord hanging down along the wall, and the open mouth of the man sleeping in the other bed, and asked for a sign: 'Give me a sign,' he has repeated to God, whom he has now begun, after the black-eyed man's arrival, to call Allah. 'Insh'Allah, give me a sign that will lead me to carry out Your will.'

He can't catch his breath.

He doesn't know yet what he must do, but he knows that he is ready. He has been ready for as long as he remembers. Maybe since childhood, when he did not yet understand what this was about. He has been ready to take on his Assignment, to step forth and die, if he must. He is ready in the same way as the young men and women who curl up around bombs and blow themselves up in crowded buses and bazaars. He has been ready for anything that will let him die for something bigger than himself. It often seems to him that there's been some mistake. That he should have been born a Palestinian or a Chechen, and that all his problems stem from the fact that he was born in an affluent Nordic country where you cannot become a hero by blowing yourself up.

Joona reads the announcement one more time and turns away. He walks to the balcony with slow steps, so that no-one will notice the difference. He could rise up off the floor and float around like a helium balloon, over the hospital roof and the city. Joona lights his cigarette at the wrong end, spits out bitter leaves, lowers his head and crosses his hands against the balcony railing. 'Thank you, dear God,' he whispers and presses his forehead against the chain-link fence.

28

'Hide me! I ran away from the hospital, and the cops are looking for me and… Dear sister you have to save me!'

Joona had lost weight. I could feel the curves of his ribs through the hospital bathrobe and the sharp edges of his shoulder blades against my hands. His pupils were cloudy and he had red rings around his eyes, his chin was unshaven and he had drops of yoghurt in his moustache. Around us the people had stopped chanting and had turned to look at us. A young girl whispered something to her friend and they covered their mouths with their mittens and giggled. I pictured myself pulling a gun and shooting both of them in the forehead.

'Come.'

I wrapped my arm around Joona and started leading him through the crowd. He leaned on my shoulder like an old man. Ian walked behind us without saying a word. When we got past the demonstrators and into the park, Ian took off his jacket and put it around Joona's shoulders.

'Thanks,' Joona said, and looked at Ian as if he'd seen an angel. 'I really appreciate it.'

Joona and Ian had never met. That was my fault. I was so happy with Ian that it seemed like an abomination, an insult to Joona. I was also afraid that something in our happiness would shatter if Joona became a part of our world.

Ian looked at me as if he knew what I was thinking. When I led Joona to the side of the road and called a cab, Ian stood a little way away from us. He was only wearing a thin sweater and had stuffed his hands under his armpits to warm himself. He looked adorable, understanding, lost, and alone, and I would have liked to put him in a bottle and hide him in my breast pocket, so he could always hear my heartbeat and nothing could ever hurt him. He was still standing in the same position when the taxi came and I got Joona into the back seat and climbed in next to him and knocked on the window and mouthed the words 'Call you later. I love you.'

In the cab Joona pressed against me.

'You won't let them take me, will you?' he asked. I said no. His hair smelled of grease and dandruff. He laid his head on my shoulder and mumbled vague things about how in the hospital he had drunk some cleaning fluid from the cleaner's cart, been sent to have his stomach pumped, and then escaped in the morning before the doctor came by to see how he was doing.

133

Sleet slid down the taxi windows. I stroked a sweaty spot on Joona's back and remembered him as a small boy in the black car, that day when Father drove too fast. I wished I could ask the driver to take us out of town and due east, across Siberia to China or the Russian Far East. That I could let Joona fall asleep in my lap and trust the car to ferry us without stopping through snowy birch forests and the desert where the skeletons of dead animals rise up through the endless sand like statues. I wished I had the money to spend the rest of my life with Joona in the steel shell of the taxi and watch the whole world flash by our windows.

'What on earth were you thinking?'

Joona was lying in bed. He had on Ian's flannel pyjamas and his eyelids hung halfway over his eyes.

'I wanted to set myself on fire,' he said. 'Like the Buddhist monks. First I thought I'd do a suicide bomb inside the American embassy. But I couldn't set that up in time.'

There was not a trace of irony in his voice. There never was. It was one of the most straightforward things about him. He meant everything he said.

I tried to imagine what would have happened if he had had time to do it. How he would have flamed up like a human torch amongst all the people, and how the smell of burning flesh would have spread through the crowd, stopped the shouting and set nervous whispers in motion. I remembered a Czech man who immolated himself in a Prague square the same year our parents met. And another man who immolated himself in the same square just recently, after sending out a message to the whole world over the internet condemning the Iraq war and general apathy.

'Why?' I asked Joona in as calm a voice as I could manage, so as not to hurt his feelings.

'It would have been so absolute,' he said. 'To fight killing by dying. Everyone would have had to wake up. I've thought about it a long time.'

I mixed up some juice in an old plastic cup that we'd used on outings when we were kids. Joona half sat up and drank. He held onto the cup with both hands, like a child. I thought of the surge of people at the demonstration, the families with children, the old women and boys and girls in dreads. What would they have thought if Joona had had time to carry out his plan? How annoyed they would have been, for a long time afterwards. We. How annoyed we all would have been to have our demonstration co-opted by a man hearing vague voices in his head and seeing things no-one else saw. Nobody wanted the protests of an escapee from a mental hospital. For some reason this is what affected me most strongly. My

Joona's dream would never come true. His final act would stop no-one.

I didn't even dare think about what would happen if he were to keep his dream of the suicide bomb alive and somehow carry it out.

I took the juice cup into the kitchen and threw a second blanket over Joona. He looked innocent and helpless under it. I wondered how he could have done something requiring that kind of planning. How he had thought of the cleaning fluid. How he had found his way out of the hospital in the morning. Had he had his own matches?

'No,' Joona said when I asked. 'I forgot them in all the hassle.'

I smiled.

'Maybe it was a good thing you found me?'

For a moment he looked as if he were about to smile back. Then he pulled the blanket over his mouth and sighed.

'Thank you,' he whispered. 'For being on my side.'

I stroked Joona for a long time after his eyes fell shut and his body twitched on the verge of sleep. I listened to the neighbour's clock, which chimed every fifteen minutes with Big Ben bongs, I looked at his pale cheeks and shaving cuts and saw a little boy on a summer's day in the back seat of a car flashing international finger messages to the cars behind us.

When his face had relaxed into sleep and his breath came evenly, I crept into the hall and fished my mobile phone out of my handbag.

'You're searching for a Joona Louhiniitty,' I told the businesslike female voice that picked up at the police station, 'who escaped from the hospital and his involuntary psychiatric committal this morning – well, he's here with me at this address.'

When I'd hung up I went out to wait for the squad car. It was cold. I was only wearing jeans and a T-shirt, with Ian's broken old tennis shoes on my feet. I pulled the shoes off and pushed my feet into the slushy snow. The cold bit into my skin and I remembered Joona years ago after his first release from the hospital.

'Don't let anybody take me back there ever again!'

Joona had lain in bed in the fetal position and we had sat around him, Father, Mother, and I. Joona had gnawed his knees and wrists with his teeth and sobbed and wept so that it sounded like there was someone else trapped inside him.

'There was this old man who crept up to my bed at night and put his hand in my pyjama bottoms and. The nurses didn't believe me when I told them and. I said I'd kill the bitches and. And I didn't mean to hit them but they didn't believe me. And then but. They strapped me to the bed. I was there all night. All night strapped to that bed.'

Mother and Father had glanced at each other. Father's chest had swelled and a shiny sheen had covered Mother's eyes. We had stroked Joona's head, arms, and back. I had kept my eyes on the light golden hairs on the backs of Father's hands, Mother's two diamond rings, and the cracked black polish on my fingernails. 'This is my family,' I had thought and felt something cold moving behind my breastbone. There we sat, my family, joined by a bond that no-one else in the whole world knew about.

The squad car drove into the yard with its lights off. 'He's sleeping,' I had said on the phone in a desperate voice, swallowing tears. 'If he wakes up too soon, he'll try to do something to himself.' I gave my keys to the female cop, who had dimples and a ponytail and was no older than me. 'Second floor, first door on your left. The bedroom is right off the hall and… If it's all right with you, I won't come in.'

When the police had gone inside, I ran back behind the building. I sat down on the ground and pushed my bare feet into the wet snow. I pressed my face into my knees and covered my ears with my hands so I wouldn't hear Joona shouting. 'Dear Joona, forgive me,' I repeated over and over.

Blood pounded behind my eyelids. 'Dear, dear, sweet God. Let Joona understand. Don't let anyone hurt him. Give him something good. Let him forgive me. Dear God. Dear Joona. Forgive me.'

But when I heard Joona shout, when I heard the cops' tight voices and the slam of the car door, I knew that I would never, ever be forgiven.

29

The waitress brings me a Campari and wipes the coffee stain off the table. She smiles at me as if I were anyone, any ordinary woman on any ordinary day. I smile back, order a mozzarella salad and dry white wine. I'm the kind of woman who sits in a café in the afternoon eating salad and losing myself in a good book.

I go to the bathroom, rinse my eyes with cold water, brush my hair, and apply some mascara. In the bright light my face looks like someone else's. I reflect on how different it looks in the morning, in the dim light of the mirror in the lift, and how different when reflected off the café window. Do others see my face the same way I do, or is there something in it that is just for me? Do all faces have features that their owners see differently from others?

When I return to the table, my salad has come. It smells of basil and tomato, and a little wine vinegar and oil has been sprinkled on top of the white balls of cheese. The wine is cool and dry, and when I slosh it around on my tongue I can imagine I'm someone else.

I'm a self-confident woman waiting in a café for an unknown man. He has a dark suit and a scar on his finger. A moment ago he has seen her on the street from his car window, opened the window and suggested they meet. She has glanced at his finger and seen a large dusty apartment, a lonely man cutting sushi, the sharp knife and the playful motion with which the man presses the blade against his skin. She has given him an encouraging smile and nodded, waved her hand at the café.

The man comes into the café a moment later, when the woman's wine is half gone. He sits in the chair across from her and his leg touches her shin. She puts her fork on her plate, takes the man by the hand and leads him out into the rain-swept street and into a hotel, from whose upper-storey windows you can see the whole city.

They undress each other in front of an open window, explore with fingers and lips the bumps and soft bends and scars in their flesh. The door is locked and the hours pass slowly. The woman and the man get to know each other as if there were neither language nor rules, as if they had met in an empty world, where neither had a past or a future or gut-wrenching responsibilities. Nothing but the afternoon light and a body that finds ever new ways to reach out to another.

30

'Darling. What happened? Sweetheart.'

We were sitting on the bathroom floor. I had bloody cuts on my wrists. Ian put his arms around me. He smelled of outdoor air, smoke, and beer, and I pressed my face into the rough wool of his sweater and bit him through it on the chest. Ian pulled me to him with both arms and held me so long that my breathing slowed down. When I raised my eyes I noticed that his eyes were red with crying.

'What happened?'

The question burst out of both our lips at the same moment. I shook my head and put my face in Ian's neck.

'You first.'

Ian cleaned the cuts on my skin, washed my face, and led me to bed. Outside the window the morning was paling from grey to white, I threw my leg over Ian's hips and listened to what had happened to him after the demonstration.

'When you and Joona left.'

'Joona had your jacket.'

'Yes.'

'And you were cold.'

'Never mind. When you left me standing there. It felt like. I was all alone.'

After the taxi had sped out of sight, Ian had stood there in the same place for a long time, hugging himself with his hands in his armpits, listening to the hum of the demonstration echoing across the park. He wanted to talk to someone. Wanted there to be someone he could call, who would hear the tone in his voice and say sweet baby come to me, take a cab, I'll pay. Wanted a friend whose sofa he could collapse on, who would offer him a glass of wine or some biscuits or cold spaghetti and understand the taxi driving off, the strange city and his loneliness, and the war and the demonstration and the guilt that began nowhere and ended nowhere. And that continuous choking nothing that pressed him so hard on the inside that he had to fight to make the air flow through.

Because he didn't have a friend like that, Ian decided to find a *place*. He decided to walk through Helsinki until he found his own roof. A place where he could forget himself.

Ian walked past the demonstrators with his hands in his pockets, his shoes wet from the snow. A girl in a ski cap running straight towards him bent down and twisted around to escape the hand that was trying to stuff wet snow down her back. A boy that came up to Ian's waist asked him for a cigarette, the boy's friend followed a passing woman's behind with his eyes and stuck out his tongue, the woman turned and gave him the finger.

Something in all that made Ian even sadder. He closed his eyes and saw the same kind of demonstration in his own city, the skyscrapers climbing up to the heavens and the shouting human worm wiggling through them. He saw the whole pounding machine of the city, the streets glowing with the lights of cars, the escalators plunging underground, the banging doors of the restaurants, offices, tobacconists, and homes. And the wide motorways and seas that joined the city to other cities and other countries. The railways, harbours, and airports were the joints that linked the cities whose every street was drawn on maps (Ian could not get over his wonder at the ease with which a street corner drawn on a map could be found in the noise and smell of an unknown city: to him the order and precision offered by maps were almost supernatural, a gift in the form of a piece of paper that could be folded into a pocket, containing far more information than just how to get from one place to another) and the cities whose streets were muddy winding paths and if you got lost in them you had to guess at the points of the compass from the sun or bribe a tired rickshaw driver with exorbitant sums or hope that some merchant by the side of the road could tell you the way.

When Ian opened his eyes, he saw the face of the president of his country. The head was enormous and had black horns coming out of its temples. Above the horns a fire was lit. It began as an uncertain blue-hearted flame and spread crackling into a tall blaze over the cowboy hat swaying between the horns and the smirking mouth.

'Destroy the Texas mass murderer! Destroy US imperialism!' The voice belonged to a slender boy wearing a grey ski cap and an army jacket. The boy shook his fist in time to his shouts, and the girl standing next to him held up a lighter as if at a concert when the band lashed into everyone's favourite.

Ian thought it unlikely that either of them would ever stand in the wet snow in a foreign country suffocating from the feeling of having been torn loose from their own and others' lives, and knowing that in the entire city there was no-one he could talk about any of that with. It seemed so unlikely that he said aloud: 'Fuck off you goddamned candyasses,' flipped off the boy, the girl, and the sheet burning on the ground, and ran out of the park with his shoulders hunched, wishing that someone in some reality somewhere might feel some twinge of sympathy for him and open up the earth beneath his feet.

My head was in Ian's lap. He was scratching my hairline so hard that if I focused on it enough I could forget my thoughts for a moment and feel only the movements of his fingertips, small circles from my forehead to my temples and down to the back of my neck.

'Are you listening?' he asked.

'Of course.'

An image flashed before me: a bent-over man on a slushy path, behind him a column of smoke rising from a burning flag. A second image at the same moment: a child rising from an upstairs bed driving his plastic three-wheeler across the hall to our parents' bedroom, the rumble of the wheels on our ceiling and Mother getting up to take him in her arms, to yank him off the three-wheeler despite his resistance, the child's shriek and Joona's shriek when he opened his eyes and saw a young police officer beside his bed. No.

'Go on, darling. Scratch harder. My scalp. Make it hurt.'

Temple, nape of the neck, back of the head. A twinge of pain when Ian wrapped a wad of hair around his finger and pulled.

'Harder.'

Not Joona. No. Ian alone, walking shoulders hunched towards the shore, turning around and running to the shop to buy some beer. Litre bottles. Two full plastic bags. And the children watching him come out of the shop, whispering: 'That wino, maybe he'd buy for us?'

Ian ran to the shore with the plastic bags in his hands. He sat on the icy granite and looked out at the surging sea, the fortress rising gloomily on the island opposite, and the lights of the ferries to Sweden in the mist. He opened the first bottle. He drank the warm beer in long gulps, some spilled down the sides of his mouth onto his neck and inside his sweater, turning freezing in the cold air.

He drank more and let out a burp or two, long and loud as when he was a boy, back when they had contests where everyone had to burp his own name. Ian always won. He could burp not just his own name, Ian Brown, but Ronald Reagan, Johnny Rotten, and Marilyn Monroe. The same boys who the day before might have dunked Ian's head in the toilet bowl or locked him trouserless in the girls' bathroom, were reluctantly respectful of his prowess at burping, and asked him to burp things like cunnilingus, motherfucker, and fucking nigger.

Ian drank a second bottle, and a third. When he stood up,

the world swayed around him as if someone had turned the camera. He braced himself on the back of a park bench behind him, sucked his mouth full of air and swallowed. A bubble of air swelled up in his throat. Ian pushed it out in a noisy burp, shaping it with his lips into the words 'Ian Brown'. A passing couple with a pram turned to look at him with their eyebrows raised. Ian swallowed another bubble of air, threw his arms out to his sides, and burped: 'Fucking Finland.'

A laugh burst out of him from down around his hips, Ian dropped to the ground, opened a fourth beer bottle and guzzled down the now-cool liquid, but choked on it, coughed, hiccupped, laughed with tears in his eyes, holding his stomach. When the bottle was empty he stood up again and burped in succession:

'The US sucks.'

'War sucks.'

'Finland sucks.'

'Saddam sucks.'

'Ian Brown sucks, sucks, sucks!'

The last *sucks* hurt his chest, brought an acidic taste of vomit up into his throat. Ian swallowed it back down, sat on the bench, and pressed his head to his knees. He wrapped his arms tightly around his legs, but the world around him swayed. It swayed like the carousel in the park when he was a kid, when his stomach turned and he wanted off but the carousel wouldn't stop, the horses, elephants, and chickens kept spinning, the lights attached to the ceiling flashed and the music played. And as it had back then, dread now crept into his mind. What if this never ends? What if he never finds solid ground, can never walk straight ahead at his own pace, his stomach calm and his thoughts clear? What if this all just goes on and on, Mother buys cotton candy from a pale clown and waves smilingly at him over the pink cloud but never comes to take him off the ride?

Ian fished his mobile phone out of his pocket and held down number two. *Hi, this is Anna. Sorry I can't come to the phone right now, but please leave a message.*

Ian called over and over: 'No big deal, hi Anna no problem.'

And: 'I'm not drunk, see, I've just been thinking some things over.'

And: 'Please! Come get me pleazh!'

And: 'Answer. Please. Answer.'

After listening to my outgoing message for the ninth time, Ian wiped his face on the arm of his sweater, drank the last bottle of beer, and held down number three on his phone. He squinched his eyes shut, waited through the transatlantic delay, listened to the faint beeping, and thought of a weave of cables running on the ocean floor, one strand of which carried the message he'd sent with his thumb like a flash of light across the ocean to his native land, which almost seemed imaginary to him by now. When a voice at the other end said sleepily *Hello*, for a moment Ian was unable to say anything. Only when the voice at the other end threatened to hang up did he whisper: 'Mom.'

Sober, he wouldn't even have considered making such a call. He was distant and polite with his mother, and although he didn't particularly enjoy her company or miss her when he was away, he did sincerely and painfully wish her happiness. If he hadn't built a whole world out of his father's happiness, he probably would have wished her happiness more than anything else in the world. Ever since childhood he had assumed that he couldn't expect anything from his mother. He considered it his task to take care of her, or at least to make sure that he didn't cause her any more worry. He never thought that she might have something to offer him.

So he later found it hard to figure out what he was hoping for, sitting there on the shore, listening to that distant voice through the phone's speaker.

'Maybe you were hoping for a Great Encounter,' I

suggested. My eyes were shut and Ian's finger was moving between my eyebrows.

'Yeah,' Ian said. 'Maybe.'

He said no more, but when I imagined him alone on that shore, clutching the phone against his ear, I believed I knew what he had hoped for. I imagined him as a small boy with a mixing-bowl haircut and an embarrassed expression and believed that he wanted her to hear that boy's voice. I believed that Ian hoped his mother, waking on another continent in her expensive nightgown and her hairnet, would remember the little boy who came home from school with his hair wet and said, swallowing tears: 'Everything's fine.' I believed that he hoped his mother would remember that boy and understand how hard it was for him to say those words. And maybe he hoped his mother would whisper that she knew how that boy felt. That she did remember that boy, and all the other boys, Ian small and bigger, with peach fuzz on his upper lip. That she knew and remembered it all and that Ian wasn't alone, that he could come home any time and she would take him in and know who he was.

It didn't happen. His mother sounded sleepy and irritable and could not understand why her grown son would call in the middle of the night, too drunk to speak in complete sentences. Ian heard Michael waking up, heard her covering the receiver with her hand and having a fuzzy conversation behind it, a conversation ending with the words: 'Are you going to tell him?' 'What, now?' 'When, then?'

The words sobered Ian up. His palm squeezing the phone against his ear was sweaty as he whispered, or perhaps shouted:

'Tell me what? Mom. Mom!'

Ian heard the scratchy sound of his mother handing the phone over the bed to Michael. He heard the sound of a throat being sleepily cleared, then a man's friendly but distant voice saying the words he had been expecting, fearing, and imagining in his mind ever since he stood at the airport check-in counter with his laptop and his overweight luggage.

'Ian, your father died two weeks ago. I'm sorry. Truly.'

31

'Your mother is very worried.'

He takes off his cap and sits across from me. His ears are red and his hands are cold, and the coat he hangs off the back of his chair smells of outdoor air.

'How'd you find me here?'

'I called Ian. He said you like to sit here. He's worried too.'

He orders a glass of sherry and lights his pipe. In his black alb with the closed front and white Lutheran collar he seems to be from another world. Behind the clay twist of his pipe a very human minister, a shepherd among his sinful flock, a sinful man of God. Sin. How silly it sounds. We were taught in confirmation class that sin separates us from God. I raised my hand and asked how so. Isn't God a self-centred narcissist who created humans in his own image and then, without even offering any alternatives, decided to punish those who did not love him? Isn't God more brutal and egotistical than any dictator?

'Is that what your father thinks?' the minister asked.

'Fuck if I know,' I said and walked out, biting my lower lip. I walked down to the shore and threw little stones into the swaying reeds. I listened to the whisper of the wind in the reeds and dreamed of the beautiful writer who walked into the water with a stone in her pocket. If only I were as bold, I thought then. If only some day I could be as brave as she.

Now Father is sitting across from me and I have to concentrate in order to be able to talk to him. Under the table I keep clenching and unclenching my fists. I can't fall apart. Not here. I can't do anything that would undermine the conventions that tell us who we are, what I've grown up to be and what our relationship is. When was the last time he and I were alone together? When did I last see Father outside the hospital, their place, or church? What do I know about his life? How is it possible to live with someone all the way to adulthood and then grow so far apart that nothing remains but an annoying awareness of shared memories?

Father pushes the remains of my salad around on the plate and looks at once lost and out of place, like old teachers outside of school, or old boyfriends anywhere. I look out of the window and try to think of something to say. A red car is pulling into a parking space on the curb. The car door opens and a young man with sunglasses on his forehead gets out and I remember a red car from many years ago. Father and me and the day that was almost truly happy.

It was the day of my high-school graduation. Father took us to a Russian restaurant to celebrate. I had on a dress bought at a flea market and had dyed my hair red. Joona was in a suit he'd borrowed from Father. He had washed his hair. He sat across from me and chatted and smiled so that his teeth gleamed. Father and Mother held hands across the table.

'Just no big family gathering,' I'd said, and Mother had protested, almost as if she'd really wanted one. Father had given me the thumbs-up sign. 'For that,' he'd whispered, pinching my cheek, 'you get the world's greatest gift.' I had folded my clothes on the bed and thought of my own home, into which I'd soon be moving, quiet mornings and turquoise walls.

Spring smelled better than ever that year. I walked in the streets with my jacket open and thought of the autumn and years to come. I hadn't applied for the university, because I wanted to be free for a while to do whatever I chose. I wanted to know how it felt to sit on the window sill in my bathrobe, watch the people head off to work, and then plop back into bed.

For dessert we had baked ice cream frosted with meringue mousse and fresh strawberries. I ate it with my eyes closed. The sweetness of the strawberries spread onto my tongue and the ice cream flowed coolly over it. 'Like taking a bite of heaven,' I thought. A man dressed as a Cossack and a woman wrapped in a boa sang Russian songs with melancholy tunes and lyrics that I couldn't understand.

When we'd finished the ice cream and the musicians had left, Father banged his knife against the side of his glass.

'Anna,' he said. The sun coming through the window lit up the corner of his eye and made its dampness glisten. 'Your mother and I are unbelievably proud of you. You've graduated from high school with top marks on your matriculation exam. To tell you the truth, there were times when we were a little worried about you, whether you'd have the strength to do it all. You had to go through so much. Some things that we'd really rather have done without.'

I glanced at Joona. He was drawing circles with the base of his champagne glass and smiling as if all were well. Father cleared his throat. 'You showed that you are capable of studying under pressure. You showed us that when you decide to do something, you do it, all the way. We are very happy about that and… we wanted to give you something special.'

Father and Mother stood up. Mother straightened her

dress and picked crumbs off Father's suit. 'Let's go outside,' Father said. His cheeks were flushed and he was smiling with the excitement of a child. 'Let's go and see what's out there.'

I followed Father and Mother outside. Joona stayed at the table smoking a cigar. Father had let him choose the most expensive one off the menu. The waiter had brought the cigar to the table on a tray and snipped off its end with silver scissors. Savouring it, Joona looked like all the other men in the restaurant, affluent and a little world-weary. The waiters treated him the same as everyone else, and that made me happier than anything else had that day.

Outside it was bright and almost warm. We squinted our eyes and coughed in the dust coming off the road. Father whistled '*Gaudeamus Igitur*' and walked a few steps ahead of Mother and me. When we rounded the corner of the restaurant, he told me to close my eyes.

'Open 'em!'

We were standing in the car park behind the restaurant. Mother squeezed my hand and her ring pressed into my skin. It hurt, but I didn't pull my hand away.

The car's bright red body gleamed in the sun. Its seats were white leather and a card in the shape of a student cap was taped to the back window. The edge of the card was like the cap's peak, and in the middle it said in golden letters:

For Anna. Congratulations and love for all your journeys. Mother and Father.

I looked at the car and the card. Father and Mother looked at me. I took a breath.

I'd seen the car before, in a photo in Father's car magazine. 'This is what I want some day,' he'd said. He had lain there on the sofa with the magazine on his stomach and flipped through the pages dreamily. 'Saab 96. A Finnish beauty.' The car was photographed in the autumn in front of an old house, with fallen maple leaves on its roof and a cat next to the front wheel. Father had looked so happy that I had tried to act interested. I'd asked about the model and the price, although I couldn't understand him dreaming about old cars.

Didn't he remember the same as I did? That sunny day, that trip that was supposed to end well? The wind rushing by the windows, the cars streaking past, and the blood that coloured his chest hairs red? If he didn't remember that, what did he remember? If he didn't remember, why did the events of that day invade my thoughts in the small hours through my dreams or in the daylight in the middle of a random conversation and make me blush as if I'd done something embarrassing?

When Father had asked what I wanted for my graduation present, I hadn't said anything. What I wanted most of all in the world was a trip to India, but I was sure it was too expensive. I didn't want them to have to say no.

Father and Mother looked at me expectantly. The car stood there gleaming and sun-warmed and the card in the back window flopped a little. The car was at least as expensive as a flight to India would have been. It was more than they could afford, and yet they'd bought it for me. I didn't want the car. I couldn't imagine what I'd do with it.

'Wonderful,' I said. 'Thanks. Great gift.'

Father put his arm around my shoulders. Mother's ring dug into my skin. I filled my lungs with dusty air and hugged them both at the same time, as hard as I could.

Back in the restaurant we had coffee and cognac and small hand-made sweets. We ate and drank and spoke of the summer and the autumn and about how quickly I'd grown from a little girl into an adult. No-one said anything unpleasant or raised their voice. We ate, drank, and spoke like any group of people who liked each other. Like any family celebrating their daughter's high school graduation.

After coffee, Father gave me the keys to the Saab.

'Enjoy,' he said, and patted me on the back.

'And call when you need help moving.'

'Don't drink too much,' Mother said and hugged me too tightly.

'Congrats, Sister,' Joona said and raised his hand as if planning to hug me.

When I drove the Saab out of the car park, they all stood there waving after me.

That evening the school's new graduates took the ferry over to the Klippan restaurant to celebrate. We danced to slow songs from the eighties, drank red wine from glasses and the hard stuff we'd brought straight from our own bottles. The evening was warm and beautiful and before we left we all sat on the granite side by side, held hands, and sang 'Youth Tango': *My warmth and my love I give to you, Beautiful is my youth*. The sea rolled black and cold and the Kaivopuisto park lights across the way glittered on its surface.

The evening was warm and thick with longing, but I felt none of it.

I lay in my party dress on a thin mattress on the floor of my new apartment, drank cheap wine straight from the bottle, and watched as the moonlight spread in squares across the floor.

Now Father is sitting across from me and wants to know why I haven't gone to the hospital to visit Joona. My Father, with webs of tiny lines around his eyes and grey in his hair. My Father. A little boy naked in the snow and all the other boys about whom I know nothing.

And now. I can't cry now.

'What is it?' he asks. 'My little Anna.'

I can't help the storm that begins in my belly and rolls over me in hot streams to my cheeks, and becomes a trembling that is totally out of place. Not now. But it rolls over me, and his voice is the same as back when we were kids and I was the child who sometimes resembles me still. Suddenly I am that child.

'It was my fault,' I whisper.

'What was?'

'Joona.'

'What?'

'That evening. The demonstration. It was my fault.'

32

'Your father died two weeks ago.' Ian lay next to me on the bed. He had an arm laid across his eyes as he mimicked Michael's voice. 'I'm sorry. Sorry? Thanks. Wonderful. Fuck you.'

I thought of Ian's father. A man I didn't know, who'd died alone in a nursing-home bed. I wanted to give Ian his father as he'd imagined him. The biker hero who built houses for the wounded. I wanted to dive into his family's history and find something in his father's life that would open the world up to Ian. I had to settle for stroking the fuzz on his shoulder and the stubble rising up from his throat.

'You want to talk about it?' I asked carefully. Ian rolled over onto his side and pressed his face against his knees.

'Not now. There's nothing I know how to talk about.'

He squeezed himself into the fetal position. I felt an icy belt at the pit of my stomach. A tall man in that position looked scary, unfit for this world. His body trembled as if from extreme cold. He asked me to talk about my evening. 'Why the hell are your wrists all slashed up?'

From somewhere in the house I heard distant shouting. I remembered an article I'd read about relationship violence and wondered whether something was happening right now that would destroy someone's life. If I got up from the bed this instant and crept into the hallway to determine the direction the shouting was coming from, and maybe even the reason, could I keep something terrible from happening? Or was the sound coming from a couple making love, rocking somewhere on the other side of time and sinking their nails into each other's flesh?

'Did you hear?' Ian asked.

'What, that shouting? You heard it too?'

'No. I want to know what happened to you.'

I pushed the corner of the blanket into my mouth. I wondered how I could possibly find the right words. Where I could find the words to tell him about the strangle grip under my breastbone and the fact that I had no clue of how I should live after tonight. Since there were no such words, I rehearsed the evening's events in fragmentary sentences. I told him about the sleeping Joona and the cops and how I walked to the shore after the squad car's lights had melted into the darkness.

★

There was nobody at the shore. A wet comic book flapped at the edge of the water, next to it a down-at-heel man's shoe. I knelt near the water and took the shoe in my lap. It was dark brown suede, size 43, Ian's size. It had yellow stripes down its side and its shoelace was broken at one end. I lifted it to my face and sniffed its scent of sweat and sea water.

I was testing the temperature of the water when my mobile rang.

I imagined myself walking into the water with the shoe in one arm and the phone in the other hand. I imagined the phone under water, how quickly the water would destroy its sensitive parts so that only my voice remained, telling people to leave a message or call me back later.

It was my mother calling.

'Where are you?'

'At home,' I lied. 'What's up?'

'Joona.' Her voice cracked.

I clutched the shoe against my neck.

'Are you guys at home?'

'Yes.'

'I'll be right there.'

Father met me at the door. His eyes were swollen and he had a half-eaten sausage sandwich in one hand. When he saw me he spread his arms. We stood there for a long time in the doorway saying nothing, my face against his sweater.

'I'm glad you could come,' Mother said. She was sitting at the kitchen table sewing a button on Joona's old bathrobe. She had a half-empty coffee cup and a tub of melted butter in front of her. I put the butter in the fridge and washed the knife. Father and Mother followed my movements with their eyes. For a moment they seemed like two children who had broken something valuable while playing and were waiting for an adult to come to decide what to do.

I asked them if they wanted a cup of tea.

I put the mugs on the table and boiled water in the whistling kettle that Joona and I had bought Mother for Christmas many years ago. Well, I'd bought it and Joona had promised to pay half. At some later date when he had money.

'Joona's in intensive care,' Mother said. She stabbed herself in the finger with the needle. The blood left a brown stripe on the waxed tablecloth. I tore off a piece of paper towel and bent over to wipe it up. 'Tried to kill himself.'

Father sat half bent over the table squeezing the mug in his hands and slurping boiling hot tea with his brow wrinkled, now and then emitting short grunt-like bursts of air.

I'd known it. The knowledge that something like this would happen had lived inside me for much longer than just that evening, as long as I could remember. When Mother told me what had happened after the squad car had pulled out of my courtyard, I saw it all. Not as a new image, as an old one. I saw it like an old dusty painting left behind in some back corner of my mind, now dusted off so that its surface shone brightly.

Joona sits bent over inside the cold ribs of the police car, pressing his forehead against the window and looking up at the violet-red sky. The sky is the same colour as the paintings of that Russian painter that he and Father used to go to see long ago.

The cold buckles bite into his stomach. He doesn't want this. Doesn't want to think of the squad car and the hospital he's been rushed to against his will. Or the warmth that flowed into him from his sister's hands just a little while ago, the feeling of connection, the feeling that he was safe. Or the anger and dread churning about inside him. Or the images of his sister that he keeps seeing, where she's holding an axe above her head and bringing it down on his head, splitting it open right at his parting. Such thoughts push up something black and deep. He has to keep it at bay.

He just wants the Russian artist's sky and the delicate scent of dust in the gallery, Father's arm around him and the paint- ings where wooden ships rock on red, purple, and green waves. He remembers the paintings he liked most. The ones where the sea was stormy and the ships' sails were torn to ribbons. He remembers Father's arm on his shoulders and the peace that made it possible for him to plunge into the world of the paintings, to smell the sea salt, the icy billows and the sailors' dread when the horizon goes black and the waves break over the deck. He was at one and the same time a weather-beaten man desperately reefing sails and a boy standing quietly in front of a painting, who knew he could turn away at any time, knew that his Father was standing there big and strong, ready to take him to the museum café and buy him a drink or an ice cream.

As the squad car curves past the park into the hospital yard, Joona is once again between two worlds. One is an experimental world. Home, the squad car, and the hospital's top-locked doors are part of an experiment into which he has been sent from somewhere else. And somewhere far away is the world where his true home is. There his thoughts stop flapping and whatever is messy and painful clarifies.

Home. Somewhere far away, in a place he doesn't even know yet, is his home. He failed to perform the Assignment. Nothing went as planned. But maybe that was how it was meant to go. Maybe that was part of the experiment. Maybe it's time to return home.

Joona's hand clenches into a fist and the blood pumps in a vein in his neck. The car stops. Two cops grab him to pull him out. Joona keeps his eyes on the ground. There's a red gleam in the whites of his eyes. Outside the car he manages to wrench himself free at precisely the right spot, to kick the male policeman in the groin and smash both hands through the window and tear, tear his wrists on the sharp broken glass so that the blood sprays onto the cops' faces, his bathrobe, and the snow. He keeps shredding his wrists against the broken glass, and despite the pain there is joy in his eyes. He's going home now.

'Is he going to be OK?'

'Probably.'

I stroked Mother's hand. Father set his tea mug on the table. Both of them looked at me. I wanted to lie down on the floor on my back and sob. Bellow that it's my fault. I wanted Father to take me in his arms and pull me so hard against his chest that I wouldn't fall into that black gaping pit that seemed to be opening under my feet. There was something else I wanted. It was an ugly and scary wish. The kind you don't say out loud. I wanted Joona not to wake up. I wanted him to have killed himself. I wanted the life that had twined us together to end that night.

But when I looked at the bent-over figures of my mother and father, the tea mugs that reminded me of the Saturday evenings of my childhood, and the faces that distantly resembled my own, I knew that nothing would end for a long long time. It was my job to keep them from falling apart. I had to do something that would keep my parents from turning before my eyes into forgotten old shells or tiny helpless children. Something that would carry them through this night and the weeks, months, and years to come, as long as they would live.

'We'll get through this,' I said. I squeezed their hands. 'Joona will be taken care of. When he comes home he'll be better than before. Everything will get better. I'll help you. I promise.' I got up from the table and pulled Father and Mother up with me. 'You two need to sleep so you'll have some strength tomorrow morning.' They followed me into their bedroom. I could almost smell the medicinal and naphthalene scent of the hospital, feel the bumps on the soles of the nurses' health sandals on the bottoms of my feet.

I pulled back their bedspread and fished under their pillows for their night clothes. Father had an old-fashioned pair of pyjamas Gran had bought him, with gaping holes in both armpits. I stood by the window looking out while they changed. In the garden stood the same Schwedleri maple tree in which I'd hid from Joona when I was a child, and behind it rose the granite on which I had fallen many times and scraped my knees. It felt strange that I'd lived in this house most of my life. That I'd lived so close to them.

When they were ready, I tucked them into bed. They lay there with their backs to each other. Father stuffed yellow earplugs in his ears. Mother asked me to bring her a glass of water to put next to the bed. I brought water for both of them and turned off their light. 'Sleep tight,' I said, and patted their shoulders through the blanket. 'Everything's going to be fine.'

After I closed the door I heard Father's quiet voice. 'Thank you.'

'No problem,' I whispered through the door and pulled on my shoes. 'We'll call when we wake up!'

I ran down the stairs in the dark, holding my breath, as if someone might step out from behind a corner at any moment and lay a heavy hand on my shoulder. I clenched my keys in my fist and ran out of the front door straight into the street, into the night-cool air and the dark-splitting glow of the streetlamps.

33

Anna Father Mother and maybe the world,

I've Understood something. I don't know if you can Understand. Or if it even matters. But I'm writing anyway.

I have to try to live. Inside my head. And outside. God didn't take me away. Was he on my side or against me? It's not enough that I walk against time. I have to try to live.

Have I lived a difficult life? Do I have a right to hate? I've been reading something and Understood: Hate has nothing to do with Right. That's irrelevant. This isn't a game and you can't tie the score. You have to try and calm your head. Try to live.

Psychosis is a word. Suffering isn't. There's just an intolerable dread of existence: you'd DO ANYTHING to make it stop. Eight anti-psychotic drugs and a hospital that's supposed to 'treat' you. But the world of suffering is a grave. There's no coming over to this side. You have to try to live. Is it possible?

Why live when you can't live anyway? That's the crux of the crisis. Middle age will come. Old age. Death. My life is inside this head. I'm trying to stay on the charts. Somewhere everything will settle into a bigger picture. Maybe.

I can't conquer suffering. I can't avoid life. I try to think of time as a landscape. You have to walk through it. When you get to the edge it's over. At the edge there's Light. My life is a journey towards the Heavenly Light.

Love,
Joona

34

Father's alb is rough against my cheek. The fabric smells of tobacco and old-fashioned aftershave. Father has grown fat and fragile, but his arms are firm around me. I squeeze my eyes shut. There's nothing but his arms and the softness of his chest under my temple.

I'm very small. So small that I have no idea who I'm becoming.

'So there would still have been something.'

It was some day after the demonstration. I don't remember much about those days. I just remember the weight on my stomach and the nights Ian and I spent awake, fingers clutching fingers. The silence between us and the hesitant sentences we framed in an attempt to share all that had happened that evening and that night.

Maybe it was some Sunday afternoon, when we had taken a long silent walk and stopped at the shore to watch the sea melting into ice floes. Maybe that was the afternoon when Ian sat on a rimed rock and started to talk about everything his father's death had awakened in him. Maybe it was at precisely that kind of moment that he flipped up the collar on his jacket and uttered the words that Father's alb is now reminding me of.

'Although the thing is, everything was so clear. What his world had become. And that he'd never get better. Though I'd tried to live and accept it, still. Somehow I was sure. That death wouldn't be like this. That a person can't just stop existing like that. Life can go any which way. Death can't. Though I never thought that out consciously. Something in me was sure that there would still have been something.'

Maybe Ian raised his hands to his mouth then, and blew on them to warm them up. And I pulled his hands into my own mittens, he felt the scars on my wrists and asked me again why. Maybe that was the moment when I looked past him to the children scraping at the icy snow, to the swans that had returned too early, and found the first words.

'Because Joona survived. And none of his dreams will come true. And it's all a part of my life.'

Maybe it was that evening when we caressed each other to sleep and slept for the first time in a long time the soft sweet sinking sleep of the dead.

'It was my fault,' I whisper again, my lips against Father's rough alb.

'I feel the same way,' he says. He speaks quietly, as if to himself. 'Every day. That it's all my fault. What happened to Joona. And to you. Although all I wanted was… that everything would be OK for us.'

He's never said any of this. We've never talked about it. His words blow a wind through me.

I open my eyes and see his teeth. Between his lips flash short stumps. When I was small and had a nightmare I would crawl between Mother and Father to sleep, and I would wake up to a grinding noise. I saw my sleeping father's profile through the dark that dripped through the blinds, the sheen of sweat on his brow, and the fierce movement of his jaws.

'Henri grinds up in his mouth everything he's running away from,' Mother explained when I asked why Father chews at night. I imagined Father's mouth full of tiny goblins, whose tail hairs got caught between his teeth.

Now those stumpy teeth flash above my head. Father looks at a bread crumb on the table, the half-empty glass in his hand, the thin bracelets jangling on the waitress's wrist. He speaks as if praying or thinking out loud.

'Would things have been different for Joona if I had been

different? Did I steal my own child's life? That weighs on me every moment. How do you even begin to beg someone's forgiveness for something like that?'

I pull away from him gently, so as not to disturb the process going on in him. I study the book while he finishes his drink and puts on his coat and hat. I can't say anything. Not now.

What he wants to say is connected to all the ones who are already dead, it's connected to his own boundless feeling of good luck and daunting, crushing success.

I keep my eyes on my book and say nothing. We aren't yet ready to have this conversation. Maybe we never will be. But even if the moment never comes, I know now, this moment, with the book's page under my palm and my eyelids swollen with crying, that the words exist. There are words that will help us get through what happened. And forgive.

'I'm going to the hospital,' I say. 'Tell Mother that I'll be there before visiting hours are over.'

'Thanks.' He pats me on the shoulder and walks out. His black alb peeks out from under his coat. He walks like an old man.

35

When I leave the café it has started to rain. The sky is reflected in the puddles on the street. I stand in one of those puddles at the edge of the zebra crossing and remember how Joona and I stood in puddles as kids, holding hands and closing our eyes and diving through their surface.

On the other side of the puddle was backwards land, where you walked with your feet in the sky and waved down at the earth. You slept all day and stayed awake all night, the adults played tag in the yard and the children leaned out of windows to boss them around. Meals consisted of ice-cream cake, chocolate pudding, and boats made of sweets, and dessert was brown gravy with crumbled potato on it. You could take as many toys from the shop as you wanted, and the shop owner gave you money whenever you did. Presidents waged war by having fistfights and everybody was given free food. The most food went to the African children, who rested under palm trees, fat and happy drinking milkshakes mixed by white servants.

There's a hole in the sole of my shoe and the cold water wets my socks and toes. The cars going by throw muddy water on my trousers and I look at the reflection in a puddle of a woman who could be someone other than me.

The woman is my twin sister in backwards land. She has the same kind of glasses that I wear, hair straggly from the rain, and a denim jacket with a frayed hem.

The woman has a bag over her shoulder with a Dictaphone, a novel, and a laptop in it. She's spent the entire day in a peaceful café, watched the dogs and the grey-haired women walk by. She has tapped the laptop's keys with quick fingers and written her story for the paper. After that she sighed contentedly, ordered a mocha square, and opened her novel.

Life. London. This moment in June. This moment in April. This moment, she has thought, and stroked the book's surface. How sad if someone were to kill herself without knowing that moments like this exist.

The woman is on her way to visit her brother. The thought of seeing him again fills her with joy. It's wonderful that there is a person who is almost the same age as she is and who has known her for her entire life. It's wonderful that there is someone with whom she can examine her memories.

My twin sister meets her brother in the white hospital in

backwards land, the hospital where the doors are open round the clock and blossoming shrubs grow in the garden. The hospital is an ordinary place where visitors smile and carry flowers. When the patients leave they are healthy and full of energy and get on with their lives just like anyone.

My twin sister lifts her hand at the exact same moment I do. She smiles. Her face is smoother than mine. She is happy that I'm just a reflection in the puddle. An imaginary twin sister in an imaginary world that she will never need to set foot in.

36

Anna,

Thanks.

    Thanks sister for coming to get me from the hospital yesterday.

I was afraid of people. I had decided not to be afraid, but still. How do I stand among People when for the longest time I've only seen Beings and Specialists?

    Thanks for coming. Thanks for the ice cream. It tasted totally good. The same as the sea smells. Totally good.

Now it's night and I've got my head in my hands as always on sleepless nights. I'm waiting for the pain to start. From somewhere the thought comes to me: what if it doesn't come? Maybe it won't come tonight.

    Your brother,
    Joona

Acknowledgements

The author and publishers gratefully acknowledge permission to reprint copyright material in this book as follows:

Os to telos I [To the End I] by Miltos Sachtouris from the collection *To Skeuos*. Copyright © 1971. Reprinted by permission of Kedros Publishers.

The Letters of Virginia Woolf, vol. 5, 1936–1941, published by Hogarth Press. Reprinted by permission of The Random House Group Ltd.

'The End' (Morrison/Krieger/Densmore/Manzarek) copyright © Doors Music Corp. Reproduced by permission.

'The One' (Hetfield, Ulrich) copyright © Metallica. Reproduced by permission.

'Nuoruustango' ['Youth Tango'] (Kaj Chydenius/Anu Kaipainen) copyright © Kaj Chydenius and Anu Kaipainen. Reproduced by permission.

Mrs. Dalloway by Virginia Woolf. © 1925 by Harcourt, Inc., © Copyright renewed 1953 by Leonard Woolf. Reprinted by permission of the Society of Authors, the literary representative of the estate of Virginia Woolf.

For news about current and forthcoming
titles from Portobello Books and for a
sense of purpose visit the website
www.portobellobooks.com

encouraging voices,
supporting writers,
challenging readers

Portobello
BOOKS